final grades

final grades

ANITA HEYMAN

75756

DODD, MEAD & COMPANY
New York

YA
F
Hey

Grateful acknowledgement is made to the following for permission
to reprint previously copyrighted material:

Sidgwick and Jackson for the extract from "Choosing Shoes"
by Ffrida Wolfe.

"GLORIA"
(English Lyric to GLORIA)
Original Words and Music by GIANCARLO BIGAZZI & UMBERTO TOZZI
English Lyric by TREVOR VEITCH
© Copyright 1980, 1982, by S.p.A. MELODI
Casa Editrice, Milan, Italy.
Sole Selling Agent Sugar Song Publications, Inc. and Music
Corporation of America, Inc. New York, N.Y.
USED BY PERMISSION.   ALL RIGHTS RESERVED.

1 2 3 4 5 6 7 8 9 10

Library of Congress Cataloging in Publication Data

Heyman, Anita.
   Final grades.

   Summary: In despair that her perfect scholastic record
is about to be marred by an English teacher whose
demands confuse and anger her, seventeen-year-old Rachel
begins to question the direction of her life and the
goals that her parents assume for her.
   [1.–Teacher–student relationships—Fiction.—2.–Parent
and child—Fiction.—3.–High schools—Fiction]
I.–Title.
PZ7.H46Fi 1983   [Fic]   82-45997
ISBN 0-396-08141-X

To Dan, Alissa, Asenath, Anne
and to Donna

chapter 1

The teacher's hands dart to the stack of papers on her desk. I lean forward, an answering quiver in my stomach. But her thin fingers do not settle on the pile. Mrs. Baker is obviously not ready to present us with the fruits of our labors, our reward for hard work in the fields of literature.

"Shakespeare gets right to the point in *King Lear*, when Lear announces he is turning over his kingdom to his three daughters, and asks which loves him most. Please turn to page two," our overseer commands.

My hands turn the pages, but my face turns toward the window and the gray November sky. I'm not worried that Mrs. Baker will accuse me of loafing. She's too absorbed in Shakespeare's mellifluous phrases.

1

Sometime I should count how many gray days there are in West Gate between November and March. The slate belt, they should call it, or the sun never rises on the Connecticut coast. I can see the Sound sliding under the sky like shifting metal plates. It's my friend, my companion through many a long class. When I was younger, I composed about a million odes to the water—the swish, the rush, the slap. It's amazing my brain isn't waterlogged. Or maybe it is. Maybe that's the trouble.

I wish I were sitting on those metal plates, sliding away from the gray coast, the gray classroom, the teacher's gray, gray eyes.

"Lear says, *Know that we have divided/In three our kingdom, and 'tis our fast intent/To shake all cares and business from our age . . .*" Mrs. Baker's high, quavery voice draws me back. She seems all voice and eyes and quick, gesturing hands. Everything else fades away. Face narrow, colorless. Body swamped in a bulky brown sweater. Pale hair pulled straight back.

Like my hair. I reach up quickly to the barrette at the nape of my neck. Is that how mine looks, just shoved out of the way? Except that mine is dark brown and reaches almost to my waist. David said that it danced against my back as I walked. He said that it set off the oval of my face, a perfect shape, like an egg—the symbol of spring and renewal. I snatch my hand away. Only he didn't renew me. He shelved me instead.

"So Lear is dividing his kingdom among his three daughters. But how does he do this? What does he ask of them? He says, *Which of you shall we say doth love us most?/That we our largest bounty may extend/Where nature doth with merit challenge.* What does he mean? Cynthia?"

First-hand-up Cynthia. She'd do well on one of those TV high school bowls. First to push the buzzer. Might not know the answer, but she'd sure get to that button fast. Actually, she'd probably know. She needs to know, to be on top. You can see the shiny eagerness on her round face as she answers. A regular teacher-pleaser. So how is that so different from me? I like to please, to be on top. Only this year, I don't know how to get there.

"Lear is saying he'll give the largest share of his kingdom to the daughter who loves him the most."

"Is it the one who loves him the most, or the one who *says* she does?"

"Well, er—" Cynthia is not one for riddles.

"Rick?"

Rick doesn't even look up. He turns his pencil in his fingers and stares at it. It used to be that such behavior would send waves of superiority over me. How could someone not even try to answer? Now I know. He's a fellow victim, a sinker, a drowner. I'm even impressed by his clear absence of effort. Besides, he doesn't need to answer. All he needs is that tumble of blond hair and that long, lean body slouched in his chair. The kind of body that set me drooling in my junior high classes, when body was all and mind beside the point.

"Natalie? Look at the line. What does it say?"

"Well, Lear says, *Which of you shall we say doth love us*

most? So I guess he wants to know the truth." Natalie looks at the teacher with her Bette Davis eyes, her Shirley Temple smile, a manner that says, I know you'll find me pleasing, so why should I worry about my words? How can anyone feel such comfort with the world?

"Any other opinions? Damien?"

Damien. Of course, Damien. Damien is her natural class resource, her fount of wisdom. She doesn't have to worry that the well will run dry, that the students' words will evaporate. Damien's always sitting there with a full bucket. They have an affinity, those two, matching brain waves that just naturally wind through lines of literature, pulsate around obscure language.

"Well, what Lear says directly is how much do you love me? But when he says *tell me* and *shall we say,* I think his real message is that it's the words that count, not the truth."

Is that convoluted enough for you, Mrs. Baker? Lear says tell me, but don't tell me, but tell me without telling me. I look at the textual engineer across the aisle from me, the electrician of language. He's leaning back in his chair with his long legs stretched out, his hundred-watt position. For a three hundred-watt job, he pulls in his legs, leans forward and chops at the air with his hands.

Under other circumstances, I might even find him good-looking. He has strong, straight features, silky dark hair, and pale skin. Dark and pale. Strong and vulnerable. Sweet and sour. But in school, it's all sour. Misfit. Square peg. My enemy.

4

"And what does the line, *Where nature doth with merit challenge* mean? Rachel?"

It's dangerous sitting across from the teacher's resource. One slip of her eyes, and there they are, focusing on me. I look down at the words in my book. They scare me. The truth is, Shakespeare scares me. The great, the incomparable, the immortal Shakespeare. I've heard about him all my life in tones of awe, each of his precious words wrapped in the reverence of centuries, in the halo of the holy. It's as though there's a glow around the words that keeps me from really seeing, understanding them.

The words in front of me now are blurred, wrapped in mist. I have to grasp them, make them clear. To show Mrs. Baker that she's wrong about me, wronged me. To prove to myself . . .

Where nature doth with merit challenge. It doesn't connect with my brain. The channels are clogged. *Where nature—* Take a step at a time. Nature? Whose nature? The daughters'? Lear's? Take a stab. Plunge in. It's only painful for a minute. "It means he'll give the most to the one with the most deserving nature."

A small pursing of the lips, a slight lowering of the lids in irritation, a sliding of the gaze along its well-traveled track across the aisle. "You need to take it apart, word by word. What does *nature* mean here? What does *challenge* mean? Damien?"

Go back to your old reliable Damien. What do I care about your nature, your challenge? Give me Mr. Reese, my English teacher last year. He'd talk about nature, about Lear's nature. Why Lear was loony enough to hold a verbal contest for his kingdom. Why he had one gigantic tantrum and disinherited Cordelia when she refused to give him the flattery he wanted. That's the meaning you should be dismantling, Mrs. Baker.

"I think by *nature* he means his natural affection. And *merit* means what the daughters earn. So he's saying they have to win their inheritance by proving their worth."

Mrs. Baker doesn't have to say anything, she just sort of radiates. Damien supplies her current, her energy, lights up her life. She's on a mission, you see. She's a preacher for this textual analysis, this in-depth criticism. Go directly for the writer's words. Slice, rip, dissect. Nothing extraneous admitted, like the author's life, or the period he wrote in. None of this unsophisticated stuff like character analysis or discussion of themes. She's going to hone our minds into sharp blades for shredding texts. We'll walk out into the world true textual analysis believers.

Only, I don't find that all this dissecting helps my understanding. It stops me. I get hung up on the words, lose the flow of the story. I swim below the surface of the words, unable to rise, to see what they're about. Obviously, I'm not one of her more successful converts.

I gnaw the skin next to a fingernail. My mother impressed on me when I was little that I mustn't bite my nails. She never said anything about the region around them. I haven't done it for years, but lately I've been taking advantage of this free territory.

6

How does Damien do it? What makes him see those words so clearly and not get trapped? His ability makes me feel about two inches tall. Nibble, nibble, little mouse, who's that nibbling at my house? It's Damien, gnawing away at my ego.

Time was when I saw things clearly too, saw what the teachers wanted. Only last year I was Rachel Gilbert, straight-A student, top of the class, on the straight road to success. Just one year to go, and then on to Princeton or Harvard or Brown. God's in his heaven, all's right with the world. Then along came Mrs. Baker, and I knew what it was like to flounder. To feel stupid. The thing that scares me is, what if Mrs. Baker is the one who's right about me . . .

Mrs. Baker has recovered from her high. "All right, so now Lear's daughters have to tell him how much they love him. I want you to tell me how they answer. What sort of words do they use? Nina?"

Nina looks startled. Mrs. Baker doesn't call on her much, and then always skips over her answers. I have a theory about why she does it. Nina reminds Mrs. Baker of herself. She's a thin, frail-looking girl with a high, small voice.

"Well, Goneril and Regan, the older sisters, use very loving, flowery language. But Cordelia's is very spare."

"Yes, but can you give me some of the specific words they use. Terry?"

You asked for the kind of words, not the specific ones, Mrs. Baker. Nina gave a good answer. Why don't you tell her?

"*Love, dearer, eyesight, space . . .*" Terry spits out the words. She's giving the teacher what she wants, literally, going almost word by word through Goneril's speech. See what you get by discounting Nina, Mrs. Baker?

With her purple nails, purple velour shirt, and thin curling lips, Terry's not easily stopped. I wouldn't want to be up against her. She lives one block from me, and I know what it feels like to be pinned by that shrill voice. But from this angle, I can appreciate her. What does Mr. Reese sometimes say about my creative writing? That it works. Well, in this situation, Terry works. She's an effective weapon.

"All right, Terry. I didn't mean every last word." Mrs. Baker ventures in at the first pause.

"Oh, no, Mrs. Baker. I want to answer fully. Here's Regan. *Metal, prize, worth . . .*"

Mrs. Baker sits down in her chair. She puts her hand up to her mouth. Do you have a secret vice too, Mrs. Baker? Do you bite your cuticles? At the beginning of the year, when she came in and said this was her first teaching job, I thought she was naive, in need of protection. And she is, except in one area. When it comes to her literary vision, she's a regular laser beam. We're the ones in need of protection.

"And now we come to good old Cordelia. *Nothing, nothing.* There're a lot of *nothings. Unhappy . . . true.*" Terry finishes and looks up with a satisfied grin.

Mrs. Baker stands up. "Now I'd like someone to compare the older sisters' words with Cordelia's."

"Just like Nina said, Goneril's and Regan's are fancy. Cordelia's are plain." Mrs. Baker hasn't asked Terry, but Terry's what she got.

"You see that the older sisters refer to riches and wealth, whereas Cordelia uses words like duty and care," Mrs. Baker says quickly. "For Monday, do a two-page paper about Cordelia, analyzing her words and any words used to describe her."

The pointed fingers lift the pile of papers from her desk. Our wages. Our pink slips. My stomach feels like a crab is running around inside as Mrs. Baker scurries up and down the aisles.

The first paper I did for Mrs. Baker, on a poem by Wordsworth, came back with a large red C scrawled on it. I hadn't gotten a C on anything since I was about two. A sensitive reaction, it said, but not an analysis. My grades have climbed to B's, but my papers come back with punchy little comments like, "You sometimes shape a good sentence, but your writing needs to be more precise," or "You need to think more deeply about the images," or "It's not clear what you're getting at." It's like the papers have sprung up and slapped me. Putting words on paper has always been something I've felt sure about. Or did.

There are quick footsteps, and Mrs. Baker's hand swings across my desk. The nails are almond-shaped and tinted pink, the only part of her that shows any care. Maybe because they're the part she sees when she anoints our papers with grades.

Like the B-minus she's placed on mine, a report on

F. Scott Fitzgerald's "The Diamond as Big as the Ritz." B-minus. Less than a B, and no comments, as though Rachel Gilbert is no longer worth commenting on. Unsalvageable. Unexceptional. Maybe not even too bright. And if she's not bright, what is she? I don't know. Without her A's, I can barely see her at all.

I stuff the paper into my notebook and throw my books together, enjoying their slap.

Damien stands up next to me, or rather, above me. He has this habit of hanging his body over whomever he's talking to. I step back. He advances. I'm going to end up in the Sound. "Say, Rachel, are you going to work on the newspaper now?"

He smiles at me, an A-plus smile, I'm sure. He can afford to be cheerful. His pale skin flushes a little. Last year Damien asked me out a number of times, but I was always with David. This year he hasn't asked. Maybe he thinks David and I are still together. Maybe he only goes out with straight-A girls. Anyway, it's just as well. I wouldn't have accepted.

"No. Maybe after lunch." Damien is about the last person I want to be with now. I turn, but then I pause. I'm just petty enough not to want to discourage admiration, even when I don't return it. I glance back and give him a half-smile—a B-minus one.

chapter 2

Nothing. No "Ms. Rachel Gilbert" on a white rectangular envelope. No address in David's clear, round handwriting. He had said it was better to make a total break, and he always was consistent. Logical, certain, consistent. I turn away from the hall table.

My mother is reading on the sofa. She smiles at me over the top of her book, her most treasured possession, her escape from the parts of her life she finds a burden, like her job. I can tell she's been home for a while. Her face is relaxed, smoothed out. "Hi. How was school?"

"So-so." In the past, I would have curled up on the peach velvet cushion by her feet, chatting, confiding. But not this year. I've learned better. I start down the hall.

"Wait a minute, Rachel. I want to talk to you."

11

I compromise. I step far enough into the doorway to see my mother's thin face and her pile of gray-blonde hair. She gets half of me, a surrealist slice. She should appreciate that; she used to paint.

"Anything special happen? What was your day like?"

"Like all other days."

She props herself up on her hand, to get a better angle on me. "Did Mrs. Baker give back the papers?"

Aha. Right to the center of her concern. "Yes."

"Oh? And how did you do?" Casual, cagey. As if she doesn't care like hell.

I shrug. "B-minus." I look at the picture over the mantelpiece. My mother painted it five years ago, before she went back to work. It's of three people at a picnic, all in pastel shades with patches of white canvas showing through. The whiteness gives the scene a kind of dazzling warmth. It's hard to believe my mother painted it.

Her face contracts, a piece of crumpling paper, a purse on a drawstring. You could say I control the purse strings in the house. "A B-minus? But you were doing better than that."

"I've regressed." I turn back down the hall.

"Well, there will be other papers." My mother's voice follows me. "It's only halfway through the semester. There's still time for you to get an A."

There's another painting in the hall. Not L. Gilbert. H. Matisse. A boy sitting at a piano with a blank expression. Behind him on a stool is a woman's figure, erect,

12

watchful, even though her face is a flat white oval. His mother. His attentive listener, or his jailer?

I drop my books on my desk and sit down, staring out the window, letting my vision blur until the dry brown branches along the fence soften into lace. That's where I want to be, out in that misty world, standing there with David. He grins at me and turns up the collar of my jacket in an affectionate, half-possessive gesture. The solid warmth of his body against mine fills up the aching absence of the past few months. I try to hold us there, but the square edges of my books jut into my image, shattering it.

I sigh and open a book. Calculus. Hard, in an easy way. Easy because it's limited. You get an answer, right or wrong. It doesn't spread out indefinitely, like an English paper, or a story, or even French literature. I suppose it's one of life's ironies that I'm good at math and couldn't care less about it. Probably a vocational test would show that I'd make a first-rate astronaut and a lousy writer.

I progress, step by step, until the problems are done. No strings attached. I survey the remaining volumes to be conquered. French, history, English, chemistry. Our teachers think we'll suffer withdrawal pains without our nightly fix. I stuff my English paper into one of my desk drawers without looking at it and pull out a black and white composition book. There's only one paragraph written inside:

"Karen watched the car coming slowly up the street.

13

It paused, as though the driver was searching for a house number, and then began to move forward again. Perhaps it was coming for her. Perhaps Michael was in it. The car pulled in front of her house, where it could stop and open its doors for her. But it didn't. It continued its gradual progress, its gift meant for somebody else."

The first paragraph of my magnum opus, my short story for Mr. Reese. He has taken a patronly interest in my writing ever since my English course with him last year, and continues to keep a critical eye on me. It's time for an expansion of my vision, he says, a full short story. Only my vision is of a feeling, a sensation of being left, of waiting, and that, says Mr. Reese, is not enough. Too vague, too difficult. I need more structure, direction, a sense of where I'm going. But what does waiting lead to? I don't know. What I do know is how to fill the waiting. I'm an expert on that. I start to write:

"Another car was coming now, this one summoned by Karen. Its red body slid in and out among the trees. Michael's car was red. But no. It would be better to make it a friend's car. It would be more of a surprise. Michael's car was being repaired, and he was so eager to see her that he had gotten Kurt to drive him. She made the car stop at her house. This time the doors opened. Michael jumped out and came up the stairs toward her with his slow panther grace . . ."

Okay so far, but now what? Two paragraphs are a little short even for a short story. What's my story, anyway? Mrs. Baker's thin sharp fingers seem to be

14

jabbing at my paper, pointing out its limitations. I push back my chair. Who says I can write a good story? Who says I can write at all?

I go into the bathroom. A calm, serene face greets me in the mirror. Full, satisfied lips, comfortably broad nose. Fake! I feel like yelling. Why don't you show the turmoil underneath? But I know why. I need a mask to slip me through life as the proper person I'm afraid not to be.

In the full-length mirror, I am a more rounded five feet six than is fashionable. David said he liked the curve of my hips, the way I carried myself. That it made me look aloof. It was when I lost that aloofness that he began to withdraw. I just held on tighter, like the time my father let go of me in deep water when I was little and I clutched him around the neck. Every time I grabbed him, he pushed me a little further away, until I was closer to the side of the pool than to him. But with David, there's no safe side.

I turn away from the mirror. I feel as cold as the bare white tiles of the bathroom. It wasn't my surface that lost David. It was what was inside.

"Any mail today, Laura?" My father smiles at my mother across the kitchen table.

"Not from Bobby, if that's what you mean." My mother digs her spoon into her grapefruit.

My brother, Bobby, is the missing member of our family, the empty set, our Elijah. Four years ago he became a fugitive from college, skipped the country, and hasn't been seen since, except for two years ago when we met him in France. He writes every few months and calls two or three times a year, but it sometimes seems like he's never lived here.

My father crosses his arms, hugging himself. With his short, stocky body and full head of distinguished silver hair, you might think he's the tough one in the family. But it's my tall, thin mother who understands how to handle Bobby's defection. If one egg turns out to be rotten, use the next. Unfortunately, I happen to be the one and only next.

"Well, I have some good news," my father says quickly. "That young woman we've been trying to get is coming to Yale."

My mother looks up. "Oh, really? You mean that economist from Wisconsin? She's awfully young to be an associate professor, isn't she?"

"Twenty-six. She got her Ph.D. from Princeton at twenty-three. She's really very able."

"She probably graduated from college at three," I contribute. Nothing like feeling sibling rivalry with your father's colleagues.

My father laughs. "Not quite. But she's impressive. Anyway, Laura, this means we'll be able to go to that conference in Puerto Rico next November."

"What are you talking about, Thomas? You know I can't get away from school then."

My mother is a secretary in a junior high, and she has about as much love for it as I do for Mrs. Baker. My father is the ogre in this scenario. If he got a job in

16

industry instead of in a high prestige, low-paying institution like Yale, she wouldn't need to work. I'm a bit of an ogre, too, for having reached college age. On the other hand, she envisions me in only the most expensive universities.

My parents discuss Puerto Rico in November. When I won't be here any longer. When I'll be somewhere else. I can't picture the house without me, my parents without me. Suddenly I'm jealous of the ease with which they are discussing their future *sans* children. Me, who has always longed for a show of unity between them.

"Speaking of next year, Rachel, when are you going to fill out your college applications?" My mother turns to me. "They have to be in by the end of the year, you know."

"I know!" How could I not be aware of those fat booklets lying on my desk, waiting for me to stamp my value on them?

"You keep saying 'I know,' but you only have five weeks left. When are you going to get to them?" The drawstrings start to pull.

"Soon."

"What's the problem, Rachel? If I could apply to college at fifteen, you should be able to do it at seventeen." My father doesn't look up from the chicken he's devouring.

That's the problem. I'm not fifteen and applying to college. My math teachers don't ask me to teach their classes. I'm not a Merit Scholar, an 800 leaguer in the

College Boards. I remember all his stories well. I learned early what sort of achievements are needed for me to feel pride in myself.

That's why Bobby left home. He knew he wasn't you, Father. He was defeated before he began. He had to get away from his failure.

"I still don't know why you won't at least apply to Yale. You know you'd have a good chance there."

"No."

"Too close to home, is that it?"

"Right." But not in the way you'd understand.

I pick up my plate. "That's all I want. I'm full."

"Then why don't you take this time to work on your applications?"

My mother's words wrap around me like long wet sheets. I struggle to get up.

"Daddy and I will do the dishes, dear. You get to work."

I put my dishes in the sink and turn on the water. My job, my nightly employment. Kooky as it is, I like the warm feel of the water, the cozy reflection of the room in the darkened window.

My mother gets up and pushes me away from the sink. "Go on, Rachel. I said we'd do them."

I can't believe we're arguing about my wanting to do the dishes. I swing around and march out of the room. But I don't go to my bedroom, site of my eagerly waiting applications. I head for the den and the indolent sins of the television. If my mother's so adamant about my not doing the dishes, I won't.

18

As I pass my parents' bedroom, I catch a glimpse of blue curly waves on paper. One of my childhood paintings, preserved by my mother in tribute to that short period when she thought I might become a great painter for her. Until it became clear even to her that the pictures in my head did not amount to much on paper. Until she magnanimously expanded her horizons to include any kind of daughterly greatness. I go into the den and flick on the bright hypnotic glare of the television.

chapter 3

I hurry up the alley, the quickest way to the bus stop. I'm in separate little pieces. My shirt is pulling out of my jeans, my jacket's unzipped, and my hair is sifting loose around my shoulders. I'm as well put together as the Scarecrow of Oz after the Winged Monkeys pulled out his straw.

I got up late this morning, on purpose, because I knew I had to get up early to start my Cordelia paper. The one that's due today, Monday, at ten o'clock. An hour and a half from now. An hour and fifteen minutes from the time the bus gets to school. The bus I'm about to miss. I feel unscrewed from myself, unscrewed from my life. With true Gilbertian logic, the less time I have, the less I give myself.

I dash out onto the sidewalk. The corner where I

20

usually meet Terry and Susan is empty. We're supposed to meet at eight-fifteen and it's eight-thirty. The bus stop is a block away, around a corner. I can't see whether it's inhabited, whether there's life. Where there's life there's hope.

Ah. A dark patch against the pavement, which grows into the ample shape of Bert Wisner. And Terry's skinny figure. And Susan's taller one. And the bus, which has appeared at the top of the hill with a charging roar.

The bus and I reach the stop at the same time. Except I am on the other side of the street, and there's an unyielding line of traffic going both ways. I rock on the sidewalk, ready to spring. I can't miss the bus when it's right there, five yards away. I wave frantically at the driver, but he stares straight ahead, chewing his cud.

One by one, the figures on the sidewalk disappear into the blue body of the bus. I feel like Ping watching his aunts and uncles and forty-two cousins disappear into the wise-eyed boat. And where will I hide if I miss it? In the yellow waters of the Yangtze River?

There's a break in the traffic on my side. I dash into the middle of the street. Cars honk. The traffic is two-way again. I hold my book bag tight, my body straight, feeling like a hunk of baloney in a meat slicer. God, I'm going to get myself killed over an English paper.

The bus huffs and closes its doors. As it noses out into the line of traffic, I run in front and pound on the door.

It opens with a resentful groan. "That's no way to

make the bus, young lady. You almost got yourself run over."

I look away from the driver's disapproving face and walk quickly to the back. I want to settle into a corner, straighten my rumpled insides, but Terry is there, expecting instant feedback.

"Decide to play hooky today?" Her small green eyes peer at me from under her baseball cap, and she crosses her chartreuse sweat-panted legs. Unlike Mrs. Baker, Terry does not fade away.

"I only wish." To play hooky from Mrs. Baker. From you. From all those expectations hovering around my head. From my own expectations.

"Slave away all night over Baker's paper?"

"Not exactly." I slaved away for about fifteen minutes, trying to find the perfect sentence to start my paper, a precise, well-analyzed sentence, loaded with textual references, that would bring Mrs. Baker kneeling before me in homage. Then I stopped. So here I am.

"Oh, you mean you whipped it off in ten minutes?"

"I didn't do it, Terry."

"Didn't do it? Not any of it?" The penciled eyebrows shoot up. The first time in recent history I've taken Terry by surprise. I'll have to remember the technique.

"Nope."

"My, my. The perfect Miss Gilbert, falling down on the job."

"All right, Terry." I look away from her sharp face. A face that can laugh when her mother tells her she wishes Terry would run away from home. I can't compete with that kind of malice.

"When are you planning to do it? She'll give you an F if you don't get it in."

I shrug. "Homeroom, I guess."

"You're going to cast a shadow over Mrs. Baker's life if you don't do it." Terry presses her hands in prayer in front of her unprotruding chest. "Ah, Shakespeare, how do I love thee? Let me count the ways."

I laugh, willing to enjoy her sarcasm when it's directed the other way.

The bus stops and a thin, washed-out looking girl gets on. A boy near the front offers her his seat with an elaborate bow. The girl sits down with no acknowledgment of his mocking manner.

I turn to Susan. "Why's Keith being so gracious?"

Susan leans toward me, her long kinky hair swinging like unbraided yellow rope around her face. "I guess it's gotten around. Letty's pregnant."

"Oh." I look at the back of Letty's stringy blond hair as she stares out the window. I don't know her very well. We've had a few classes together, but we move in different crowds. "Who's the father?"

"Rick Morgan. They're getting married this winter."

I think of Rick, examining his pencil in English. So he's dived under the whole problem, swum away, found an island. He really has absented himself. What does he think about with Shakespeare as background music? Jobs? Children? Sex?

"What a way to start a marriage. Seventeen and with a kid." Terry flicks a bony shoulder.

"Oh, I don't know. It's not so bad, if that's what they want." Susan the light-hearted. Susan could have ten papers due tomorrow and still be nonchalant.

I, of course, take Terry's darker perspective. How scary. How limiting. What a cop-out. And yet, for a moment, I see the comfort of it. Everything's settled for Letty. In a few months, she'll be married and a mother. Each step will follow the next without any decisions on her part. She won't have to stare into the empty room of her future and try to fill it.

Unfortunately, it seems unlikely that I'll get pregnant between now and English.

Nine o'clock. Fifteen minutes left in homeroom. Fifteen minutes between me and an F. Actually, I feel released. You can't do an in-depth textual analysis in fifteen minutes.

"Cordelia says, *Love, and be silent.* She shows her love in her reserve."

"May I have your attention?" the P.A. system squawks. "Please note the following announcements . . ."

"She refuses to tarnish her love by flowery statements," I write, noting only that there will be no time-consuming assembly.

"Guess who called me last night? Richard . . ." Two girls are whispering behind me, but I can't listen. I'm working against the black hands of the clock.

"The more extravagant her sisters' comments are, the

24

plainer hers get. She knows how much theirs are worth."

The first class buzzer tears through me. Darn. I haven't even written one page yet. I'll have to finish in math.

As I hurry down the hall I know I'm not doing what Mrs. Baker wants. But how can I go digging through Shakespeare when I have to conceal him on my lap in math class?

"First, I want to go over the homework on the derivatives of the trigonometric functions," Mrs. McKinley announces.

I lower my pencil to my lap. "Unlike her sisters, Cordelia refuses to beg. What she cares about is the truth, not wealth. In a way, she's a balance to Lear's excesses."

"The derivative of the cosine of x . . ." Sines and cosines scatter around me, close by, but no direct hit. Every once in a while I glance up with my best wide-eyed look of absorption.

"Let's go on to the chapter I assigned over the weekend, the chain rule for derivatives." Mrs. McKinley turns to the board.

I flip pages. I'll have to pay more attention now. As I turn back to the paper, my arm sends my math book crashing to the floor. I swoop down for it, trying to conceal the underground activity on my lap.

"Rachel, how would you find the derivative of the sine of x^2?" Mrs. McKinley's brisk voice skewers me while I am upside down between chairs. Perfect aim.

I come up panting, math book in one hand, other hand grabbing for Shakespeare, who's slipped between my knees. I'm a splitting seam, a shifting fault in the earth. I try to pull myself back together. "Since the derivative of the sine is the cosine, and the derivative of x^2 is $2x$, the answer is $2x$ times the cosine of x^2." A few kids laugh. Someone even applauds. I sit numbly, in an advanced state of shell shock.

Mrs. McKinley smiles. "Very good, Rachel. That's how well everyone should know this work—even upside down."

For the next twenty minutes, I sit in utter concentration. As the end of class approaches, however, one fear overtakes the other, and I return to my moonlighting. I need a conclusion.

"Just as Lear doesn't want to hear the truth from Cordelia, he refuses to see the truth as well. He doesn't want to see the true nature of his children; he sees only what he wants them to give to him. If he had listened to Cordelia, she might have saved him." I scribble my name across the top of the paper as the buzzer sounds.

"I thought it might be interesting today to read some of your essays aloud." Mrs. Baker looks at us with innocent eyes, clutching the papers she's just collected to her bosom.

Fraud. Trickster. You get our papers up there under false pretenses and then expose them. I want to go up and snatch mine back.

"I won't have time to read them all, of course. I'll just

26

pick some at random." The delicate fingers probe the pile, feeling for soft spots. In a loose-knit brown sweater about three sizes too big, she looks like a small child. Her sweaters range from beige to brown, and seem to come from the same rack. Her skirts are all beige. For all I know, they're the same skirt.

I lean back in my chair, willing my paper away from the searching fingers.

"All right, here's one."

I scan the lined paper for a sign that will separate it from me.

"'Cordelia's speeches are mostly very brief. *Love and be silent. . . . Nothing, my lord.* Actually, she speaks very little in the play.'"

Silence, blessed silence. The silence of words that are not mine. The silence of the Sound beyond the window, plunging and gliding in noiseless performance. I let my mind float with the water, thoughtless, aimless, the teacher's voice a dim hum in the background.

"I'd like to have your reaction to this paper." Mrs. Baker's voice raises, takes aim.

"Yes, Damien?"

Damien, of course, has been paying attention. His mind never drifts away. "It's good as far as it goes. The author could have used even more of Cordelia's language as examples."

"Yes, the paper would have been stronger if the writer had referred to the text throughout. She passed over the words spoken about Cordelia by other characters. There's a lot to be mined from them."

27

So it's a she. I look around to see who might be the recipient of all this encouragement. It could be Marjorie, who is looking wilted. But then she always looks that way, with her wide, loose mouth and shapeless body. Or Terry. She's not looking defeated. She sits bone straight, ready to do battle.

Mrs. Baker again mines the pile. Something shiny catches her eye. She pulls it out, sets it aside, and bores deeper. Maybe she thinks she'll discover a whole precious vein.

I'm entered in a raffle I don't want to win. Withdraw my ticket, destroy my number. Mrs. Baker slips out another paper and starts to read. "'Cordelia says, *Love, and be silent*. She shows her love in her reserve.'" The words cluster around my head. They won't shake loose.

"'She refuses to tarnish her love by flowery statements.'"

It's my paper! I lose. The words close over my head, deafening me. I struggle to rise, but I can't.

The trick is to act nonchalant. No one must know it's mine. I raise my head, looking directly at the small mouth casting out toads, snakes. I try to remember what I wrote, but my mind whirrs separately, like a disconnected gear.

The mouth stops. The paper lowers. "And what about this paper? Would you say it's a good example of critical writing?"

Terry shoots five purple nails into the air. "You said the last paper didn't have enough reference to the text.

28

Well, it had a hundred times more than this one. This had one at the beginning, and then zilch!"

Caught in Terry's defensive maneuver. So the first paper was hers.

Mrs. Baker nods. "What kind of paper is this, really?"

Damien extends his long arm. Always so helpful. "Some of the things it says about Cordelia are interesting, but it's a character analysis."

"That's so, Damien. The paper has some good ideas, but it's not a discussion of Shakespeare's language. It's not textual criticism."

Mrs. Baker places the paper on the pile. The detritus of weak minds. She picks up the one she's been saving and starts reading.

"'Cordelia's character is presented through contradictions. She's best described by the King of France when he says she's *most rich, being poor,* an *unprized precious maid.*'"

Go no further, Mrs. Baker. There's no contradiction in what you've done. Saved Damien's paper for the climax, the pièce de résistance. The gem in your crown. You knew it would glitter without even examining it.

Damien slumps in his chair, looking disgustingly modest. Mrs. Baker finishes reading and puts the paper down. "What do you think of the way this student has handled the subject? Does this paper have a good critical approach? Rachel?"

I stare at my desk, drilling my anger into it. No, it's a rotten approach. It's a dry puzzle. Where's the flesh and

29

blood Cordelia? I know what you're up to, Mrs. Baker. Get the misguided student to understand the techniques of the on-target one. I want to deny you your reformation, your victory. But I can't. I don't have the nerve.

"I guess it sticks to the text, if that's what you mean."

Mrs. Baker nods. See? See? That's all you have to do. Follow what I say and I'll have another convert.

I turn away from her eager face. My eyes make their silent escape out the window.

chapter 4

"ey, forget about the interview?" Damien tugs at my hair.

"Of course not!" I jerk my head away. I'd like to forget. I'd like to get away from his grinning face, to rush out the door with the other three o'clock escapees. But I can't. I have to keep pushing. I can't let myself slip any further. The gray metal of my locker vibrates as I slam the door.

"Hey, there, Socrates. Done any teaching lately?"

Drew Hudson and his twin brother, Clyde, stop, flanked by two loyal followers. Standing together in their green and gold sweat suits, they look like a small mountain of muscle.

"No." Damien stands stiffly, but he doesn't move

31

away. His tweed sports jacket looks absurdly formal. He is taller than any of them, but about half the width.

Last week in history, Damien and a friend demonstrated the Socratic method of using questions to teach. It was received about like you'd expect, with small explosions of laughter around the room.

Drew steps closer. "Explain something to me. How does old Socrates have anything over any of our teachers? All they ever do is ask us questions."

"Right on, Drew."

"We'll just start calling them Mr. and Ms. Socrates."

"Whaddya say, Damien?" Drew inclines his thick neck.

"It's not the same. They ask questions to get the right answers. Socrates's questions led his students to deeper questioning."

"No wonder the guy took poison. All those questions without answers were too much for him." At this witticism, the gang makes its graceful departure, laughing down the hall.

"The mountain people of West Gate High." Damien starts walking with a quick, jerky stride.

I hurry to keep up. "More like the old, rounded Appalachians than the soaring Alps."

He slows down and looks at me. "What are you talking about?"

"You said they're like mountains, and I said more like the Appalachians—"

"No, no." He starts laughing. "I was talking about a

tribe of mountain people in Africa in which no one gives a damn about anyone else."

"Oh. And you think Drew's crowd is like that?"

"I think the whole high school is. Everyone's always jockeying, trying to outdo someone else. They're willing to step on anybody to move up a notch."

I glance at Damien. His pale face looks easily bruised. It's true there's not much generosity in school. But he doesn't exactly do much to get out of the way.

"I'm not really clear what I can tell you for your article." Mrs. Daniels looks at us across the lab table. With her white cotton candy hair and black eyes and brows, she's a Pablo Picasso dream, a ready-made portrait in contrasts. But her mind is not dreamlike. It's direct, ready to dissect—even when the subject is herself.

"Well, the local papers said that your doctor was suspended from his hospital duties for treating you with laetrile. So that's what we want to do the article about. If you could give us some details." Damien has his notebook open, ready to catch his pertinent details as they pour out. But the details don't belong to us. Isn't illness private? Isn't cancer?

I look at the metal edge of the table, at my hands, anywhere but at the teacher. We are intruders, spies; we don't belong here. If it hadn't been Mr. Reese who assigned Damien and me to do the article, I would have bowed out ungracefully. But I need Mr. Reese in my

33

literary corner, to help me counter Mrs. Baker's punches. I need him to think well of me. Besides, why should Damien get another article under his private by-line? He's already had a piece in the local papers about students' reactions to book censorship. How many kudos does he need to line his applications?

"Are you familiar with laetrile?" Mrs. Daniels asks.

Damien nods. "It comes from apricot pits."

Damien's brain must come from apricot pits, some special substance that sops up information twenty-four hours a day. Of course, I could have looked it up too. But I didn't. I didn't want to know.

"Yes. It's not a medically approved treatment in this country. People often travel down to clinics in Mexico to receive it, but Dr. Gabriel gave it to me here. When the hospital found out, it barred him from practicing there." Crisp, clipped tones, as though she were discussing a paper. As though it has nothing to do with her.

"Why was he willing to do that? Treat you here?" Damien isn't writing. He's leaning slightly forward in his chair.

"Because of me. Because I wanted to take it. At the beginning you get a little desperate, you know."

I don't know. I don't want to know. I push aside the jar of pickled frog that's sitting on the table in front of me. "Is he still on suspension?" My voice comes out like a small yelp. "Is it a permanent thing?"

"No. It lasted four months, because he continued the laetrile even after he was suspended. He's been reinstated since."

"That took a lot of guts. He must really have faith in the treatment." Inquiring reporter Damien, going after his story with his usual intensity.

"No, he doesn't."

"He doesn't?" Damien's hand smacks the table. The frogs do a little swimming exercise in their formaldehyde baths. "He doesn't believe in the treatment, and yet he got himself suspended for giving it to you?"

"I think he felt that I had the right to take it if I wanted to. That it would help my state of mind, at least. And also, perhaps"— Mrs. Daniels's stern, proud face turns towards the window— "he didn't have that much faith anything else would help."

I want to fade away, to watch the scene from a distance, as I'm sometimes able to do. To be there and not be there, a blank film recording the scene for another time. But I can't. I'm tied to Mrs. Daniels's inky eyes, her firm voice, her scary words.

"That's pretty unusual for a doctor. I thought they protected themselves at all cost." Damien combs back his tumbling hair with an angry gesture.

"Well, I think Dr. Gabriel sees his patients as whole people, not just as symptoms. But what do you know about doctors, Damien, at your young age?"

He gives a short, sharp shrug. "My mother had cancer."

Silence. The unspoken question is answered by his closed face.

"But how could he conduct his practice, without the

35

hospital?" Damien gets back quickly to the business at hand.

I listen to them discussing the motivations and trials of Dr. Gabriel. Their words are a whirlpool, pulling me down, engulfing me.

"And is he still continuing the laetrile treatment?" Damien hammers on.

"No, it didn't seem to help. I'm on traditional chemotherapy now. At least I'm able to be here and continue teaching."

"But why do you want to be here?" I blurt out. "Don't you want to be doing something else?" Now I've done it. Performed with the delicacy of a whale. For someone who was afraid of intruding, I seem to have managed to do just that.

Instead of smashing me over the head with one of the bottles of frogs, Mrs. Daniels smiles slightly. "You mean, why aren't I traveling around the world, or living on caviar in the time I have left? Because this is where I want to be. I'm happy here with my work and my students."

I nod my acquiescence, but I don't feel it. Her words make me feel as though I'm swimming somewhere outside my body. I want to grab myself and hold on.

Julie Danby's round face peers between the swinging doors. "Oops, sorry, Mrs. Daniels. I didn't know you were busy."

Come in, come in. Don't hesitate. We need interference, relief. "Hi, Julie," I welcome her.

Julie smiles at me, her nose flaring at the bottom, as if

36

meeting her smile. I want to drag her cheerful, fresh-skinned presence into the room.

"It's all right, Julie. We're just finishing." Do I detect relief in Mrs. Daniels's voice as well?

Finishing, finished, released. That's my cue. I start to get up.

Julie hands Mrs. Daniels some papers. "Thanks for the articles. I didn't realize how many ways fish could be affected by different water temperatures."

"Yes. They're doing a number of studies at Sandy Hook Labs. I'll see if I can find any more for you." Her eyebrows move up and down in lively accompaniment to her words.

"Thank you, Mrs. Daniels." I start for the door, realizing no footsteps are padding behind me. Damien's going to squeeze out every last piece of information. He'll have it all to himself. Well, let him.

"Hey, Rachel," Julie calls out, "don't forget you're coming over today."

"Meet you outside." I push through the door, my escape hatch.

The sand slips away under our feet as we walk along the beach. I lift my face to the thick tangy air. The steady surge of the water surrounds me, like—like what? I search for words that will anchor it in my mind. Like the rustle of a giant skirt. Maybe that's why I find it comforting.

A line of seagulls has stationed itself along the beach like formal sentries. "We're on review."

Julie laughs. "More like a soup line. Hey, look at this." She stoops and picks up a shiny oyster shell. "It's a beauty. They usually get pretty broken up this time of year."

The silvery colors of the shell flicker in her hand. "What makes the iridescence?"

She brushes it off and slips it into her pocket. "The mantle of the mollusk forms the shell, and sometimes the inside layer has that mother-of-pearl. Can you imagine it? One little organ can regrow a damaged shell." Julie's skin is fresh and rosy, and her eyes are the gray-blue of the Sound.

"It's the mantle that makes pearls too?"

"Yup. A pearl is a repair job." She bends down to examine a crab's claw caught in some black seaweed. She looks so absorbed, stooping there in her baggy Windbreaker and worn jeans.

I look out over the gray water. It seems to stretch on forever, a silver ribbon rimming the earth. Something lies floating in the ripples. Something familiar. Then I remember. It was a dream I had last night. A dream that left me sweating. I was swimming through the water, swimming and swimming toward something. But I could never reach it. The water kept widening and I kept struggling.

"Julie, does the water ever scare you? I mean the way it just seems to go on until it drops off the end of the earth?"

Julie stands up and wipes her hands on her jeans. She accepts any weird thing I say and honors it with a rational answer. "No, I love it. Sometimes I think of it as my water and my beach, as though nobody else has a right to it. I can't picture myself anywhere else. Which is probably a good thing, since it doesn't seem like I'll be going anywhere." She kicks up a spray of sand.

"But I thought Mrs. Daniels was telling you the University of Miami has a good marine biology program?"

"She might as well suggest Hawaii. How am I going to get there?"

"What about your father?" Julie has lived with her aunt ever since her mother died, when she was a baby. But her father is still alive and lives across town.

"You know him. He claims he's worked hard all his life, and that he needs all his money for his old age."

She doesn't sound resentful, but I am. It doesn't seem fair. Here she is, clear about where to go, with no way to get there. And then there's me, muddy as the ocean bottom, but with parents eager to send me anywhere my little heart desires. I pull up the hood of my Windbreaker against the sudden cutting edge of the wind. My infinite opportunities seem as scary as the endless water.

"Whose mommy are you?" A three-foot-high individual with round chipmunk cheeks addresses me as we enter Julie's kitchen. Julie's aunt runs a day-care center in their house, an arrangement which does not thrill her niece.

"No one's mommy. I'm Julie's friend." Is that how I look, over the hill at seventeen?

39

"Do you know me?" A little girl confronts me, a smear of red play dough on her turned-up nose.

"I don't think I know your name."

"Come on, Rachel." Julie has made it to the stairs in one bound, the Paul Bunyan of Rose Lane. She has calculated the shortest path to her room from every point in the house.

"I go to the beach at my grandmother's. She has a blue couch." I am given the important autobiographical details; nothing so mundane as a name.

"Rachel, are you coming?"

"That sounds like a very nice couch. I'll see you later." I trot across the room, the faithful blue ox, and mount the steps to new vistas. The living room is a beach full of baby seals; they bark, waddle, wave flippers. One pushes another in a wagon, several dig into a sand table, others paint, more on their smocks than on the easels. A pleasant-faced young woman is reading to the smaller seals in the book corner, and Mrs. Danby, supervising seal, smiles up at us with her friendly face. Actually, she reminds me a little of the Pillsbury Doughboy.

"You girls look pink-cheeked. Why don't you fix yourselves some hot chocolate and join us?"

"Not now, Aunt Jen. We have things to do." Julie makes a rapid dash for her quarters. I follow more slowly, enjoying the hum, the tumble, the paint-and-popcorn nursery school smells, the just plain cheeriness.

"But Aunt Jen, why does that snail come outside its

house?" A little girl points to a snail Mrs. Danby is holding.

"Why do you think, Carolyn? You live in a house, and why do you come out?"

"To play on my swings."

I don't wait to hear how Mrs. Danby gets out of that one, but I'm sure very deftly.

"Lock the door behind you." Julie is putting her oyster shell among all her other oyster shells on her shelf. Her room is crammed to the gills with jars of pebbles and colored sea glass, clam and mussel and scallop shells, starfish and garfish and crabs and dabs and mackerel and pickerel . . .

"Afraid of an invasion?" I plunk down in an overstuffed pink chair.

"You don't know what it's like to have the house swarming with kids. They think you belong to them. If they won't stay out of my room, I won't have one spot where they can't get to me." Julie props herself up on her bed and stares out the window. Her own private peephole into infinity, a constantly changing, moving picture, reaching right out to the sky. No wonder she loves it here. "Your house is so different. With your brother gone, you have practically the whole thing to yourself."

All alone. Just me and my mother and father and their swarming expectations. "A little too much to myself."

Julie looks at me. "I forgot to tell you. Andy Klein was in school today, visiting from college. He was asking about David. Thought I would have heard through you."

I nibble my sacrificial finger. "He's a little behind the times, isn't he? You mean he didn't hear the news that David went off to college free and unfettered?" Andy was a classmate of David's. If he's home for Thanksgiving, might David not be far behind? Might he not be home already? My stomach does a series of rapid pliés.

"You still haven't heard anything from him?"

"Nope. He's a man of his word, or of no words."

"He's a thumping idiot."

I grin at Julie's totally unbiased support. I've welcomed her championing of my cause all through this dismal fall. "I won't argue with that." I reach for my paper and trusty calculus book, my most faithful companions of recent months. "How're things going with Mr. Phillips?"

"Great. He's got four chapters done. Almost ready to send it out to publishers."

Julie is helping this professor at New Haven University work on a book about the politics of pollution. He's about forty-five and balding, old enough to be her father. Seems to me she spends an awful lot of time with him, but my opinion has not been solicited, so I keep quiet.

"You sure you want to do homework? Why don't we go outside while it's still light?" Julie is frowning at her overcompulsive, overachieving friend.

"Let's just get started. I don't know how I'm going to get through everything, plus study for a history and math test, plus the utter dedication Baker expects from us."

"Maybe she expects too much dedication."

"Agreed. But she's the one who hands out the rewards."

"So? Sometimes I think you work more for the grades than because you're really interested."

I look past Julie out the window. Past the possessor of one clear, consuming interest. Past a person who doesn't understand reaching out for external certification because your internal certifier is on the blink, haywire, just plain not there.

I close my book. "Let's go out." Out, down, away. Down to the seas again, the lonely sea and the sky. Down to the only thing that lets me be.

chapter 5

"What are you doing here?" I say graciously. Damien's pale face seems to be descending upon me at every turn today, like one of the plagues of Job.

"It's not a two-person beach, you know, and I live only a few blocks away." Damien hunches his shoulders under his canvas jacket and frowns with understandable ill-feeling. "And what about you? Why'd you duck out of Mrs. Daniels's so fast today?"

"What difference does it make? I knew you'd do a sterling wrap-up." I bend down and examine a smooth disk of blue sea glass among the pebbles.

"Well, we have to write the thing up. I was counting on doing it this afternoon."

"I'm visiting Julie this afternoon."

"That's okay, Rachel." Julie is standing a few feet

44

away, stirring the still water of a tidal pool with a stick. "Neither rain, nor sleet, nor friendship . . . No, that's the mail. Well, anyway, I wouldn't want to stand in the way of the press."

"We could go over to my place. You're welcome to come too, Julie."

"No thanks. I'll stay out here until the house is clear."

"Well, Rachel?"

I stand up and slap a pebble into the placid water. I don't want to go with him. I don't want to think about Mrs. Daniels. Let him do the article, if he's so hot and eager.

But I can't let Damien have it. I sigh. "Okay, if we do a quick rough draft, then polish it at school tomorrow. I won't be too long, Julie."

A woman with long brown hair is nursing a baby at Damien's kitchen table when we come in. Young. Pretty, in a soft-fleshed kind of way. A large gray cat is sleeping on the pile of laundry overflowing the washing machine, and the sink is full of dirty dishes. The woman scarcely looks at us. "Oh, hello, Damien. Back so soon?"

"Yes, ma'am. This is Rachel Gilbert. We're writing an article together."

"Okay with me. Settle wherever you can." She lifts the baby from her breast and fastens her bra. I look away from the white uncovered skin. I'm conscious of Damien's lean figure standing near me.

The woman pulls down her Indian print blouse, puts the baby over her shoulder, and walks out of the room.

45

"That's my stepmother."

"Oh." The versatile 'oh.' Oh, how does it feel to have a stepmother scarcely older than you are? Oh, isn't it a strain on young male hormones to have her waltzing around the house nursing babies? "Do you have anything to drink?" I ask quickly.

"Sure." Damien picks up a screwdriver from the counter and pries open the refrigerator door.

"That's a unique method."

Damien grins. "The handle is broken. When things fall apart in this house, they're just left that way. In another ten years, it will disintegrate into the earth. Let's see, there's orange juice and Coke."

I look at the multicolored patches of dried food and cat hairs on the counters. "Never mind. I don't really want anything now." I have another more pressing need, but I'm not sure I'm ready to risk the Lanes' bathroom.

Every horizontal inch of chair in the Lanes' living room is covered with stacks of newspapers. More piles adorn the floor. Where does anyone sit in this house? Damien goes on to a kind of sun-room in the back and removes a few piles of *New Republics* and *New Yorkers* from the couch before plopping down.

I sit in a low-slung armchair opposite. Through my jeans, I can feel small pricks of crumbs. I cross my legs. The Lanes must have rear ends of steel. "We better get started." Started, ended, and out the door.

"Sure." Damien flips open his notebook to his duly recorded details. "It'll be a pleasure to introduce some reality to that school."

"So far today, you've disposed of doctors and schools."

"Most schools should be tossed into a garbage dump, as far as I'm concerned. All they care about is having us spout back the right answer. The idea of really letting us think is subversive. There're only about two teachers in that school worth listening to." Damien's sinewy body seems to cut right into the sagging sofa.

"You're right about Mrs. Baker. She'll only accept her own narrow definition of what's right."

"I didn't mean her. She's one of the few open-minded ones."

"She's about as open-minded as a clam!" Damien and I couldn't agree on the color of a red rose.

A tall man wearing a three-piece suit and a bow tie appears in the doorway.

Damien stands up. "This is Rachel Gilbert, sir. We're working on an article for the paper. This is my father, Rachel."

"Uh, hello." I struggle to get out of the deep chair. The man doesn't look at me.

He takes a few steps into the room. "I'm leaving on my Chicago trip now, Damien. I expect you to help Elaina with the children, and anything else she needs." He has the same long, straight features as Damien, except that his hair is lighter and his face more angular.

"Yes, sir."

Mr. Lane nods and turns toward the doorway. A little boy comes barreling through on a tricycle, knocking over a suitcase in his path. "Look out for Gargamel!" He coasts to a rest beside his father.

47

I expect Mr. Lane to be angry, but he only pats the boy's head. "Have you been watching television, Dana?" He frowns at Damien.

Damien shrugs. "Maybe he's watching at a friend's house."

The little boy grins at me, pointing to Mr. Lane. His face is thin, with a wide, comical smile. "That's my daddy."

"I know." I smile back at the only member of the family who has deigned to address me.

"I'm going away for a few days, Dana. Damien will play with you." Mr. Lane walks around the tricycle and picks up his suitcase.

Dana looks undecided whether to feel abandoned or not, but Damien steps in quickly. "Do you want me to draw a picture, Dana?"

Dana rides over to the couch. "Draw Buzz Bunny, and the 'murfs."

"I'm not up on the Smurfs, but I can try Bugs." Damien takes off his jacket. His lanky wrists stick out from his cuffs, boyish, appealing. I look quickly away, at his fingers sketching the rabbit's mocking face. That's no better. Long, graceful fingers; nails short, well rounded—not looking like they come from this house. Damien doesn't look like he comes from this house.

I concentrate on the emerging bunny, one arm curving up to hold a carrot in cigar position. Dana hangs over his brother's arm, his light hair swinging over the drawing as he wiggles his head.

Damien holds up the finished Bugs, one paw on outthrust hip, a perfect picture of bunny arrogance. His client appears satisfied. Dana jams the picture into the tricycle basket and pedals off with his loot.

"My father doesn't approve of television for children. He has very definite ideas on how to raise them. I'm the prime example of his methods." Damien grips his pencil as though ready to snap it. "I was force fed the alphabet and numbers practically before I could talk."

He leans forward, his hands on his knees. "But look, I watch my brothers. They're full of curiosity. They need to be allowed to follow it. Guided, maybe. Given opportunities. But not by jamming things down their throats."

"By using the Socratic method, you mean?"

"In a way." Damien laughs. "If I had my own school— Well, anyway, this job I have reading anthropology is really fascinating. I mean, when you read about all these different cultures— The kind of perspective they give you on your own . . ."

"What job is that?"

"Oh, I'm reading anthropology to a Ph.D. student at Yale."

I should have known Damien would have his long hot fingers into Yale. "And are you singing in their choir, and acting in their theater groups too?" I'm so big-hearted these days.

"No, but I go to a lot of their movies. Then I come back wanting to be Truffaut or D.W. Griffith." Damien grins. "I'm what the school counselor would call un-directed. I want to be an educational anthropologist who

49

makes films. My father just says I lack character." Damien's smile dies.

"Knowing what you want isn't so easy. But I know what Mr. Reese wants right now, and that's for us to get this article done."

"Sure. I guess we should start with why Dr. Gabriel was suspended, and what Mrs. Daniels told us about the laetrile."

I shake my head. "I don't understand her. How can anyone be so calm, so accepting?"

"I don't know. My mother wasn't."

"She must have been awfully young."

"Thirty-two when she died." The skin around Damien's full mouth whitens, outlining his vulnerable lips.

"I'm sorry."

"Her regular doctor never checked her breasts. The cancer was discovered when he retired and she went to a new one. By then it was too late."

"That's terrible." I want to reach over and touch Damien. And I don't want to. Besides, I would have to reach over about ten piles of magazines. "I see why you're down on doctors."

"Yes, well . . ." Damien's body slumps a little. He looks over at me. "I really should let you do this article. You're the better writer."

"Me?"

"You did some good things for Reese last year. Especially the one on the girl trying to jump a creek while all the other kids waited. What was the line? Something about imagining jumping so many times that there was no such thing as jumping."

I stare at him. "Do you remember everything you read?"

"No. Just the things I like."

Smiles inside my head, ding goes my ego. The way to a girl's heart is through her writing. "In some of my crazier moments, I have wanted to write." Why am I telling him that? One compliment and I release my most guarded secrets.

"Why do you want to write?"

Why? I've never wondered why.

I look down at my hands. My well-chewed digits. I resist their comfort. "I remember seeing these fish once in an aquarium that could see above water and below at the same time. Sometimes I feel that way, that I'm looking at things in two ways. It's a guard against boredom, anyway." I look up with a laugh.

The corners of Damien's mouth tuck into an impish grin. "Sometimes I feel that way too. Like I can see your turtleneck as just a sweater, or I can tell you that that shade of red sets off your dark coloring perfectly."

Damien's gaze feels warm and pressing. I'm suddenly aware of the curve of my breasts under my sweater. I look down quickly, hiding my consciousness. "And I can see that we'll never get this done if we don't stop talking."

But Damien does not cooperate. "Say, how about

going to one of those Yale movies with me? They're showing *The Mouse That Roared* this week."

I surprise myself by being tempted. But then Damien reaches across and flicks back my hair, and everything disappears. There's only David making the same gesture, putting his hands on my shoulders. I jump up. "I'm sorry, I can't. Listen, we'd better do this in school tomorrow. I just don't have my mind on it now." I hurry ahead of Damien toward the door.

chapter 6

*K*aren dug her trowel into the wet dark earth. The quietness of the street hummed through her like a drill. She cut into the weed's roots and jerked it out of the ground."

I put down my pencil. I know all about the dull hum of waiting. This is Thanksgiving Day. David has been home since yesterday, at least. There's nothing exciting about waiting. It's thin and drab, like still, brown water.

The phone rings, and I jump up from my desk. "I'll get it!" I dash down the hall to the den. I want my privacy, just in case.

"Hello?" Voice smooth, unruffled.

"Hello? Rachel?" My Aunt Louise's low, half-amused voice mocks me.

"Yes, Louise, this is Rachel." Rachel the unwanted, the forsaken. Louise is my mother's younger sister. She's considered the pretty sister, and my mother the smart one.

"You're sounding so much like your mother these days, Rachel, that I can't tell you apart on the phone."

I don't *want* to sound like my mother. I don't want to *be* like my mother. "Mom's in the kitchen putting up the turkey. Do you want me to get her?"

"No. Just tell her I found time to make the pumpkin pies, so not to worry."

I start down the hall. But my mother's not in the kitchen. I see her in the living room with my father. He's sitting in his armchair, holding her around her waist. My mother's hands are on my father's shoulders, pushing away.

He releases her, and she walks toward the kitchen with quick steps. My father sits staring at his hands. He looks so forlorn, I want to comfort him. Instead, I go to my room and shut the door.

I pick up a paperweight from my bookcase and shake it until the snow cascades around the tiny mountain village inside. Such a cozy scene. I have a whole collection. I go down the row, shaking each one, the swan on the pond, the Santa on his sleigh. Encapsulated worlds of cheer.

I go to my desk. Write about what you know. Use your experience. Well, I know about phone calls that aren't for you. I can write about that, can't I?

"A telephone rang inside the house," I scribble in the

54

notebook. "Karen stopped digging and turned to the porch, where her mother would come to call her. Michael wasn't driving by because he was phoning her. He was calling to say he was taking her to the party Amanda was giving tonight. She could see how it would be. He would look at her with that light, pleased smile that made her feel whole. And afterwards . . . Her fantasy went on, filling the air around her, past the time it should take for her mother to call her, past the time it could be for her . . ."

I read the paragraphs I've written. Fragments that don't move. I can't just wait for something to happen to me, and then rush back to my desk and write it down. I can see myself sixty years from now, going through life, notebook in hand, working on the same story.

My eye falls on a sketch hanging on my wall that my mother did for me of a few trees growing out of a clump of forsythia. When we were sunny together. When I trusted her to my dreams. When she was the source of my belief in myself. I feel suddenly lonely.

I go to the kitchen and stand in the doorway. She is moving around the room with short, sharp steps. "Aunt Louise called to say she's bringing the pies."

"Good. That's a help. Now if only your father would do something, instead of disappearing into the computer."

"He has work to do!" I don't want to hear her talk about him that way.

"What no one in this family seems to realize is that I have work, too."

"Well, if you need help, I'll do it," I offer in my most charmingly begrudging manner.

"No, I want you to do your homework. But your father doesn't understand that I come home from one job and have to do a second one here."

"Well, at least you get home early."

"After a day in junior high, you need time to recover. Besides the kids and the teachers, the principal seems to think I'll do half his work for him."

"If you hate it so much, why don't you do something else?" I want to rub out the frowns, cut the purse strings.

"And what else could I do?" she says with a snort.

"You could sell your paintings! People would buy them."

"I'm glad you think so, Rachel, but I doubt if anyone else would. I've told you before how hard it is to get your paintings displayed in a gallery, and how few of those sell."

"You could at least try."

My mother wipes away my words with a wave of her hand. "I haven't painted for years, Rachel. Besides, I'm not good enough."

The pale sunlight in the room contracts, as though even it cannot withstand my mother's hopelessness.

I swing away. "I'm going out."

"Where are you going?"

"For a ride."

"A ride?" She follows me out of the kitchen. "Why are you going now?"

"I need to get out."

"Well, make it short. You have a lot of work to do."

I hurry toward the door, toward bright, undefeated sunlight.

Instead of turning toward the beach, I head up the hill, past the park. At the top, I turn down a side street. The yellow shingles of David's house pull my gaze like a spot of denser gravity on the block. I drive by slowly.

The house is lifeless until I am almost past. Then the front door opens. I swing around the block, so fast that an irate driver slams on her brakes. I slow down only when the house comes into view again.

Mrs. Seldin's small round figure is heading down the walk to the car. David is behind her. They must be going somewhere for Thanksgiving dinner. David's looks sock into me with the same power they've always had. His black hair and eyes, and his slow, almost insolent walk make a dark patch of energy on the sidewalk.

So, he is home. He's home and he hasn't called. That seems worse somehow than his not writing all these months. It's like he's taken a scissors and cut me out of all the photographs of our life together.

"How are you doing, Sweetie?" My mother is standing by my desk.

Sweetie? I haven't heard that endearment for quite a while.

"Okay. I'm almost finished with this French." I don't mention my story. I don't want her to know about it.

She sits down on the edge of my bed. "Well, then maybe you'll have some time to work on your applications. It's already Sunday, after all."

That's what it is, after all. After all the time David could have called. After he must have started back to school. After a dry, dreary four days, in which even Damien didn't call. I could tell T.S. Eliot something. April isn't the cruelest month. It's November, the beginning of short, dark, dull days.

"If I do that, I can't finish my work," I grumble. "It won't do much good to apply to college if I flunk my courses."

"And it won't matter if you pass your courses, if you don't apply anywhere."

I shrug. "Take your pick."

"That's not all there is for you to do, Rachel." "Sweetie" is gone. "You need to retake the College Boards before it's too late."

"I don't *have* to take them again. Six-fifties are not exactly going to close all doors to me." My eyes slip to the stripes of my bedspread, lines of blue and gold marching straight up from hem to pillow. My mother's right. I should be taking the Boards in my senior year; I should give myself the chance to do better. But I remember how it felt last spring, looking down at the iron ledger of those test booklets. The measure of my true ability. The final statement of my intellectual worth. It felt like a metal plate had been slipped into my stomach. One try, and I could tell myself that I had an off day,

58

that I needed more experience taking them. What could I say after the second?

"Of course they won't. But they may not be good enough for the kind of school you should be going to. Think how many of the applicants to Princeton will have scored in the 700's."

"You can forget about Princeton!" I bang open a desk drawer and pull out a paper, waving it in the air. "Or Harvard! Or Brown!"

"What's that?"

"My latest English paper. My Cordelia paper. My guarantee of rejection."

"Why? What did you get?"

"A C. Not quite what the schools I should go to are looking for." Mrs. Baker gave back our papers on Wednesday, so that we could enjoy them over Thanksgiving. I wasn't surprised, and yet the C seemed to curl into me, like a corkscrew.

"Why did she give you a C?" My mother's voice is dry and grating.

"She said I hadn't done what she asked."

"But you're not a C student!"

I look away from my mother's pinched face. No, I'm not a C student. I didn't really work on that paper, right? But what about those papers where I did try, and never climbed much higher? Mrs. Baker is the most demanding teacher I've had so far. Is the truth that when I'm being judged at the highest level, I fail?

The bed groans as my mother stands up. She straightens her shoulders and smooths her sweater over her hips. "All right, Rachel. At least make use of the time you have now."

I pull the Princeton application in front of me. What does it say? The school "seeks an entering class characterized by excellence and diversity." They are looking for "an interesting and varied amalgam of individuals who will contribute through their diversity to the quality and vitality of the overall educational environment." I feel frozen into inaction before I begin.

It gets worse as it goes on. The poor college advisor has to rate you on academic motivation, creativity, self-discipline, growth potential, leadership, self-confidence, warmth of personality, sense of humor, concern for others, energy, emotional maturity, initiative, reactions to setbacks, and respect accorded by faculty. I feel like I'm being pulled thin as a membrane to be examined from every aspect. I'm surprised they don't ask for a blood smear and urine sample as well.

Then the teachers get into the act. Two of them. "If you intend to pursue a particular field of study in college, it is to your advantage to have a report from a teacher who is familiar with your work in this area." Mrs. Baker is familiar with my work in English. "What are the first adjectives which come to your mind to describe the applicant?" Ah, let's see. Imprecise. Unanalytical. "Which intellectual characteristics and abilities are most memorable?" Fuzziness, laziness, and downright stubbornness. I can see what Mrs. Baker would do to my Princeton chances.

60

The scariest parts are the essays. "Tell us more about yourself as a person . . . We seek a response which will help us to know you better." How can I describe myself to them when I can't even do it to myself? *He hath ever but slenderly known himself.* Maybe I can claim, like Lear, to be above such petty self-examinations.

What do I have to offer to prove that I'm one of the "diversified" who will add vitality to the school? A few newspaper articles, a small selection of poems and stories from past years. A story I can't seem to get a grip on this year. I try to summon myself on the paper, but the concrete things I might say crumble into nothing. Why should I help them to know me better, when it seems the only way they will accept me is if I pretend to be someone I'm not?

I stare out the window at the red house next door. It rises three stories into the air. I feel dwarfed, insignificant. How can I satisfy those lofty requirements? And if I don't, what? I only have to remember my mother's taut face to know what that would say about me. That I've been examined and found wanting. That Mrs. Baker is right about me. That I am lacking in some basic, unredeemable way. That I don't count.

"Here, Rachel. I want you to take this to school tomorrow."

I look up at my mother standing by my desk. "What is it?"

"A note for Mrs. Baker."

"A note? What's it about?"

"Never mind. I just think it's time something was

said to her. Put it with your books and give it to her tomorrow."

Time something was said? What has my mother written? But I don't ask. I take it obediently, as I did as a child when my mother sent in a note to explain an absence. I slip it between the worthy pages of *King Lear*.

chapter 7

I've read your mother's note, Rachel." Mrs. Baker turns round, childlike eyes on me.

I see the plain, cream-colored paper on her desk, framed against the green blotter. I dropped it in her mailbox this morning, quickly, without letting myself think. But seeing it now in her possession, I feel its power over me.

"I must say I was a little shocked."

My glance shoots to the floor. My skin shrinks, crawls. Shocked? What did my mother say? Why was I such a simpering idiot, a patsy, a deliverer of my own doom? I want to grab the note and run.

"Your mother seems to think that I've been treating you unfairly. Is that what you think, Rachel?"

What can I say? I stare at my hands, clutching the

straps of my book bag. That the way you want us to read seems to tie my mind in knots? That I want you to look at me as though I count? "Well, it's just that sometimes I thought my papers were graded a little low."

"I'm sorry you feel that way. Can you give me an example?" Thin lips pressed together in concentration. Ears at attention, ready to catch every vibration of my complaint. She wants to understand. This accusation of an imbalance in her methods has injured her tender teaching ego.

All I need is a perfect example of my underrated brilliance, an instance of extreme literary injustice. Only, I can't think of any. "Well, maybe the paper on 'The Diamond as Big as the Ritz.' I thought my analysis of dream versus reality was okay."

"I'm sure it was, Rachel. I'd have to check the paper to remember specific comments. Your problem is not in your ideas, which are often perceptive, but in the closeness with which you tie them to the text. You have a tendency to suggest, instead of being precise. You need to analyze, define, pinpoint, to find exactly the right word." She peers at me earnestly with her small face, as though trying to convince me of her point, to establish her rightness. This isn't about you, I feel like shouting, it's about me.

She opens a folder on her desk. "I've checked your record, Rachel, and I see that you are an excellent student." Her hands are trembling slightly as she flips through the folder. I'm surprised. I didn't know I had that kind of effect on her.

64

She is flipping over little pieces of me, my vital academic statistics. See, Mrs. Baker? You've mistaken my identity, misanalyzed me. Now you'll have to give me a promotion.

"Rachel, I'm sure it must be difficult to be on top, and then run into a situation where you're not. But, you know, none of us can be first or best all the time. It's just not the way life is. Besides, B's and C's are nothing to be ashamed of. They're perfectly acceptable."

"Not when they're on a college application," I blurt out. God, what's happening to me? Rachel Gilbert, new proficiency in asking for handouts. Latest technique for getting into a top college.

"I would hate to think that I'm being unfair in my grading, Rachel. I know I don't give a lot of A's, but I feel that I reward good work. I'm trying to teach the class good critical thinking habits which I hope will help them in college. I'm not trying to hurt anyone's future." Mrs. Baker closes my folder, her slight body very erect.

"The fact is, Rachel, your work has not been as good as some of the others in the class. I do give a few A's, you know, so I don't feel I'm out of line. It may be that you just don't read with the same concentration on the language. Whatever the reason, you have not yet given me a first-rate critical paper."

I can't sit there any longer being pinned and labeled. I stand up. "Thank you, Mrs. Baker. I'd better go now."

"Just a minute, Rachel." Mrs. Baker reaches toward me with a quick, nervous gesture. "Since your mother feels so strongly, and I don't want to be the one to mar

65

your record for college, I'll do this. If you do any two of your papers over again, I'll consider them in your final grade." She looks up at me anxiously.

I nod and hurry out of the classroom, out of the long hollow hall, the squat red building. A bus stops at the corner, and I dash on. It occurs to me that my mother's note succeeded; I have another chance. Then why do I feel so lousy?

The bus is almost empty. I sit next to a window and watch the houses and trees fly backward as the bus accelerates. If only the bus would keep going faster and faster, until it flew off the ground in defiance of all rules. What if I were simply to take this bus to the end of the line, and then take another bus, and another? Where would I end up? Florida? California? I close my eyes, imagining the release of going just anywhere, away from everything that is here.

Why did I ever take that note to Mrs. Baker? Why didn't I refuse, stand up for my rights, my dignity? But I know the answer. Just as my mother has arranged most of my life for me—the right clothes, the right books, the right values—I wanted her to arrange for me to get an A.

She arranged things all right. A little pinch to the ego, a small blow to the morale, a slight devaluing of self-worth. A succinct summing up of the limitations of her darling daughter.

I pass by the hall table without glancing at it. But I don't make it to my room.

"Hello, dear. Did you have a meeting after school today?"

I go and stand at the foot of the couch. "Yes. With Mrs. Baker."

"Oh?" My mother swings her stockinged feet onto the floor and sits up. "Did she get the note? What did she have to say?"

"She said that if I rewrite two of my papers, she'll reconsider my final grade."

"Wonderful. That means she admits she was being unfair. This time she should treat you better." My mother leans back against the cushions with satisfaction.

"She didn't admit anything. She said that she's a hard grader, but fair, and that I deserved my grades. She said that I don't concentrate on what I read as well as some of the other students." As I turn toward my room, I see the wince my words send across my mother's face, and I'm glad.

chapter 8

The teacher's voice soars, dips, pirouettes. It's pleasant like this, a lilting accompaniment to my thoughts. I make no effort to distinguish the words. Why should I? I don't concentrate very well, remember, Mrs. Baker?

From my distant vantage point, I survey the competition. A few A's, Mrs. Baker said. More than one. More than Damien. Cynthia? Her round, white face presses forward, snatching every precious word. If sheer attention can get you an A, Cynthia's got it. Okay, a prime candidate. Terry? Not even Terry would be sitting there with a thin-lipped sneer if she were one of the anointed. There's Nina. Nope, Mrs. Baker wouldn't give her an A if she were Shakespeare himself. Maybe Jocelyn. Fair-haired, fair-featured, fair-minded, in a literal sort of way. Cool. Class treasurer, used to success. What Mrs. Baker would like to be? Yep, got my third. My three textual analysis disciples.

Mrs. Baker is addressing disciple number one. I zoom in and focus. I can't miss the brilliant repartee of this mutual admiration society. "As the play goes on, the natural order of Lear's world becomes disturbed and upset. Damien, can you give us an example of this?"

Damien pulls in his legs and flips back his hair. This is going to be a goody, an all-out intellectual effort. "Lear upsets the natural order by making his daughters into his mother." What's this, a new kind of psychological complex?

Even Mrs. Baker looks unprepared for this answer. "Can you explain further? Find a reference in the play?"

Can you, Damien? I pray you can't. I pray for once you do a little hedging, a little hesitating. I couldn't find the reference. I didn't even know something like that was in the play.

But no, Damien turns the pages quickly, sure of his destination. At least he didn't spout it off by heart. "Here. Page twenty-five. The fool tells Lear, *thou madest thy daughters thy mother; for when thou gavest them the rod, and puttest down thine own breeches,*

> *Then they for sudden joy did weep.*
> *And I for sorrow sung,*
> *That such a king should play bo-peep*
> *And go the fools among."*

I look away. I didn't remember that. I still don't remember it. *And go the fools among.* Well, it's not so terrible being a fool. Not Lear's fool, anyway. At least the fool sees the truth. He doesn't lie to himself. I turn and plunge my feeble mind into the cooling waters of the Sound.

". . . another example of the disruption of Lear's world? Rachel?" The teacher's voice warbles through the muffling waters. I rise slowly toward it. She watches, she beckons, she waits. I'm no longer a vague presence in the class. I'm as vivid to her as Goneril was to Lear.

"The storm raging on the heath." That was easy enough.

Mrs. Baker nods. "Please find a description of the storm."

If it's a quote you want, a quote you'll get. I start leafing through the play, slowly, at my own pace. I will give you my answer when I'm ready, Mrs. Baker. Ah, the beginning of Lear's madness, when he runs out onto the heath. No impossible Elizabethan words, no tricky archaic phrases to catch my tongue. I'm willing. "It says Lear is *Contending with the fretful elements;/Bids the wind blow the earth into the sea,/Or swell the curled waters 'bove the main . . .*"

"Yes. And there's a perfect image in that passage for what's happening in the play, isn't there?" Mrs. Baker coaxes. This is my chance. My opportunity for promotion, for admittance to the club of the incomparable three.

I stare back. I will give you what comes easily, Mrs.

70

Baker, nothing more. I will not lose myself in the tricky undergrowth of Shakespeare's language. Think what you've already decided, that I'm stupid.

"It's *Bids the wind blow the earth into the sea*," she says quickly. "It shows the upside-down quality of Lear's world, doesn't it? And what about the phrase *eyeless rage* a few lines down? Can you relate it to the theme of blindness in the play?"

You're a slow learner, Mrs. Baker, and an optimist. You have not won me over. I look at her. "No, I can't." What did Lear say to Cordelia? Nothing comes of nothing, Mrs. Baker.

She looks at me for a few seconds, a small, nagging frown across her forehead.

"Hold up, Rachel. What's the matter with you today?"

I wait a moment for Damien, and then push hard against the door. "What do you mean?"

"Mad about something?"

It shows. Good. My anger is my armor, my shield against the slings and arrows of the world. I shrug. "Just in a bad mood."

"How about a saltwater cure? Want to go down to the beach this afternoon?" Damien is standing close to me. He looks like he's going to reach out.

I look quickly away. Among the faces bobbing past us is Letty's thin one. Placid, passive, no sign of either joy or shame. No secret message written on it for me.

Suddenly I feel pressed in by all the students march-

71

ing past, the day marching on, class after class, unceas-
ing, unchanging. I turn back to Damien. "You know
that movie you mentioned, *The Mouse That Roared?* Is it
still playing at Yale?"

"I doubt it. They usually show movies just for one
night."

"Well, do you know what they're showing tonight?"

"Why? Are you asking me out?"

"Yes." I toss my hair behind my shoulders. Anything
to get out of West Gate.

"Well, then I accept." Damien grins. "I'll check on
the movie. Pick you up at seven."

"Fine." Then I remember that it's not fine. My
mother doesn't allow me to go out on school nights.
Well, what of it? That's another good reason for going.

Damien drives down the street in small jerks. His
knees are pressed so tightly against the dashboard of the
Volkswagen that it seems unlikely he can move. "I've
only driven the VW a few times."

"Oh."

"I didn't know your father was an economist. Has he
always been at Yale?" Damien is turned toward me with
great interest. Maybe he thinks the car's headlights are
eyes.

"No, he was in Washington at the Office of Manage-
ment and Budget. We came up in '75. Damien, you
turned the wrong way. This isn't the way to New
Haven."

"No? I'd better turn around then."

He wastes no time. He drives off the road, right up on somebody's front lawn.

"What are you doing?"

Floodlights flash on and a man comes out onto his porch and begins to yell.

Damien manages to find reverse pretty quickly. "He sounds angry." Damien seems surprised.

"Well, I suppose he's not fond of having people drive right up onto his lawn."

"No, I guess not." The car is now facing in the right direction and we're bouncing along happily.

"Was your father in a high enough position to know any of those Watergate characters?"

"No." I don't elaborate. I am concentrating too hard on the road. I figure one of us had better be watching.

"Some of those guys are fascinating to watch. Like Colson, going from hatchet man to religious preacher. Or Erlichman—"

Damien swings out onto the main road without even pausing. I hear brakes squeal behind us. "Damien, that was a stop sign."

"I try to keep going. I'm not too good at shifting gears."

"I have a suggestion. Let's go back and get my parents' car, and I'll drive."

"So you want to be in the driver's seat?" Damien turns down a side street. At least he didn't try to cut through some yards.

He sits back in my parent's car perfectly happy to be chauffeured. I don't mind showing greater competence in at least one area. Besides, it seems a definite advantage to have the one who's watching the road be the one who's driving.

The movie at Yale is *Night and Day,* a truly lousy picture about Cole Porter. Every time Cole sits down at the piano to compose, the film gets sickeningly reverential. But the important feature of the movie is that Cole went to Yale. When old Eli appears on the screen, the audience comments are anything but reverential. I'll say one thing for seeing a movie in a classroom. It's not exactly conducive to in-the-dark pawing. Damien sits at studious attention. Actually, I'm a little surprised.

We come out of the movie into the large, open quadrangle of the old campus. Dark buildings rise against the sky. I feel like I'm in an old walled city.

A girl with a bandanna around her head rushes by us, and hugs a boy from behind, "Where were you today? I waited in the Commons."

"And I waited in Sterling."

"No, it was the Commons . . ." They walk off arm in arm.

The steady beat of "Fame" floats down from a window. I look up, wondering what the people listening to the record are doing, what they're thinking. Two girls in long skirts walk out of the building. "I have absolutely, utterly no desire to do anything," comes wafting back toward us.

"Well, no point in following them," Damien comments.

"Is that what you're planning to do, follow someone?"

74

"Sure, why not? They might be going somewhere interesting."

"Probably home to bed."

"Who says that's not interesting?"

I turn away from Damien's grin.

"Now take that bunch. They look like they know where they're going." Damien nods toward three boys and a girl who are crossing the campus at a rapid pace.

"Dum, de dum, de dum de dum de dum de dum . . ." Damien starts tiptoeing after them in exaggerated Pink Panther fashion.

"Is that your idea of how to remain inconspicuous?"

Damien laughs. "Come on. The idea is to get close enough to catch any verbal clues."

We jog down the walk and stop a few yards behind our quarry. With such a delicate approach, I expect them to turn around and scream, but they're talking together heatedly. "The program was a disgrace," a boy with a blue knapsack says.

"We have to get some debates. That'll attract people," the girl replies, her long earrings tossing in the lamplight.

"It sounds like they're leading us to a policy meeting of some kind," I whisper to Damien.

"No, no. A group like that is going to some out-of-the-way coffeehouse with lots of atmosphere, where they can sit and talk."

We come out of the college, onto a large, busy street. I look at Damien. "Very out of the way."

75

"Wait. Have patience. We'll probably have a long walk."

The group walks a few yards, then turns and opens a door.

Damien grins and shrugs. "Wait till you get inside. It's probably just a cover."

We walk through the door into a brightly lit ice-cream parlor. "Um, full of atmosphere."

Damien is chuckling. "Well, I didn't say what kind of atmosphere. Care for a Moulin Rouge, or a Brownie Sundae?" He reads the captions from some of the artwork on the walls.

"I'll settle for a chocolate ice-cream cone."

"I shouldn't be here at all. I'm really bushed," a girl in line in front of us says to the boy next to her. "I've been up two nights straight studying for a German exam, and the professor almost caught me snoring in my Romantic Lit seminar today." The girl has a full, pouty mouth, and leans against the wall in a weary, familiar way.

I slump one shoulder against the wall and look out on the world with jaded, half-closed eyes. I check out my loafers and tan cords. Okay. They don't give me away. My camouflage as a Yale student is intact.

The girl is looking at Damien with an appreciative eye. I see him as she does: dark, brooding good looks, poetically vulnerable face—just the thing for a girl who takes Romantic Lit. I move closer to him and smile enticingly.

He's preoccupied with his stomach, however. "How

76

about some candy?" He gestures with his cone toward the rows of tempting jars at the back of the room.

"Sure. I'll take some of those mini chocolate bars." I feel like a child on a spree. Damien pays for the candy, and I head for a table.

"No, no. Let's take a walk."

"With ice cream? At the end of November?"

"It's a warm night. You'll like it." Damien stands at the door, motioning me with his dripping cone. It appears that he will stand there until it's a puddle on the floor. I sigh and follow him outside.

"It *was* a warm night." The cool sweetness sliding down my throat is turning my insides the same temperature as the outside air. "Here, take both cones." I reach in my pocket for a more temperate candy.

"Nope. Look, there's a technique to this. They teach in yoga that at the center of your mind is a tiny sun. All you have to do to keep warm is to find it."

"How do I manage that?"

"Concentrate. Don't let other thoughts interfere. Just imagine that sun is getting larger and larger, and you're getting warmer and warmer."

"It's working already."

"Really?" Damien looks pleased.

"It must be. Look at the way my ice cream is melting."

"Oh, you." Damien laughs and pulls my hair.

We walk past the Gothic carvings of Sterling Library, down the steps to the campus green. In the dark, we are indistinguishable from the other figures crossing it. I am

77

accepted, admitted; I have embarked on my new life. "This is the way I'd like to go to college; ice cream and movies, and no work."

"Unfortunately, if I'm here next year, I think the work will be included." Damien leans back against a low wall.

"Is this where you want to go?"

"It's where my father wants me to go. He made me apply for early acceptance." Damien sounds about as cheerful as Eeyore.

"Is that so terrible? I thought you liked it here."

"It's not that. It's that my father wants me to live at home to save money."

"I see your problem."

"I don't know why he wants me home. We mix about as well as oil and water. I remind him too much of my mother. He claims I have the same impulsive nature, that I'm basically a lightweight. Well, if he's planning to keep me home next year so he can direct my life, he has a surprise coming." I feel Damien shivering next to me.

"Look, you won't really be living at home," I say quickly. "Your life will be here. You could eat here and study here. You'd just be at home to sleep." Mother confessor Gilbert.

Damien puts his arm around me. It's a nice friendly gesture. "I guess I can't exactly claim being sent to Yale is child abuse. You know, the Samoans had the right idea. According to Margaret Mead, if a teenager got fed up with her parents, she just moved across the street to someone else's house."

"I know who I'd choose for my mother."

"Who?"

"Mr. Reese."

Damien lets out a guffaw. "Rachel, you're so funny."

Me? Funny? Damien is finding a quality in me that even my mother has not seen, and that's impossible. Still, I'm pleased to have that effect on him.

"How about you, Rachel? Any chance that you'll be here next year?"

"None."

"Why not?"

"Because this is where my father is." I start to toss my half-finished cone into a trash can.

"Hey, don't you want that?" Damien grabs the cone and confronts two girls coming down the path. "Greetings, Mesdames. I have a bargain for you tonight. Two almost new cones for free! How do you like that?"

The girls grin and shake their heads. Damien shrugs, tossing both cones into the can with exaggerated Marcel Marceau flair.

"Damien, you're a nut." But I realize, as we walk toward the car, that I feel far away from West Gate.

What is the etiquette for delivering a boy to your door? Go around and open the car door for him? Grab him and kiss him? I sit in the smoky light of the street lamp, knowing that in a moment I have to get out.

Damien slides across the seat and pulls me against him. It's a shock at first. His body feels so different from David's. Less substantial and commanding. For a moment, I want to resist. There is none of the dense enveloping feeling I had with David. A short distance away, I would feel nothing.

But I don't pull away. Damien bends his face to mine and kisses me. Damien the direct. His kiss is gentler than I expected. His fingers brush my cheek, fondle my earlobe, stroke my hair. Then they're behind my neck, exploring, and suddenly my hair comes tumbling loose around my shoulders. I almost gasp. I feel suddenly undressed. Even David never did that.

I'm beginning to get the idea that Damien is not without experience in these matters. He's had other lives, lives I haven't imagined. Where is he going to take me? Will I let him? With David, that was never a problem. The demarcation line was my waist. He never tried to invade virgin territory. But the feeling was so intense, it was almost as thrilling to hold back.

Damien's lips travel to my cheek, my forehead, the curve of my neck, back to my mouth. The kiss explores my lips in strong circular currents that spin me around, down, away. Fresh, salty smell of skin, faint chocolatey mint taste. His hand makes little eddying movements down my chest. The tide inundates, engulfs me in its warm, melting flow. It laps into the hollow place in my chest, filling it.

The tide recedes, then curls under my sweater and advances again, swirling deeper. I should keep it back, on the surface of the sand. But I don't want to stop it. I want it to surge over me, to float me out of myself.

Fingers reach behind me and unclasp my bra. I feel it

80

loosen. The tickling edge of the surf runs over my skin. It caresses, plays. Then suddenly it retreats. Damien sits back and looks at me.

I jerk down my sweater, feeling more exposed by his gaze than by his touch.

"I guess I just don't understand you, Rachel. For a long time you won't go out with me, and then suddenly you ask me out and seem willing to do whatever I want. It's like—it has nothing to do with me. I just happen to be convenient."

What is this? We're pausing to pinpoint and analyze and dissect? To examine our true motives? "I didn't mean to injure your delicate sensibilities! Forget all about it!" How do you argue with dignity when you are trying to hook your bra?

"God, I sound like I'm complaining you only want me for my body." Damien covers his eyes with his hand.

I can't stand sitting there with him another second. I want to run into the house, but I have to pull together the pieces first. "I don't want you for anything. Please get out of my car."

Damien opens the door and slides slowly out. His face is partly in shadow, but his eyes look wide and hurt.

I turn away. What are you to me, Damien? Not ally, not partner, not fellow traveler. I will go on my way alone.

chapter 9

"*R*achel, what are you doing in there? Please unlock the door."

What does she think I'm doing? Writing on the walls? Having secret pleasure? I should be standing on my head in a corner when my mother walks in, instead of sitting on my bed studying for a history exam. I reach over and unlock the door.

My mother turns down the radio and sits on the end of the bed, in deference to my rottenness. "Rachel, you've hardly spoken to me for the last few days. What's the matter?"

"Indigestion." Doesn't she know what the matter is?

"Look, Rachel, I realize you're angry at me about the note. But you have to look at it the right way. Forget what Mrs. Baker said about your work. You know it's not true. What you have to focus on are the extra papers she wants you to do. Those are what count." She puts her thin fingers on my bare foot. Icy, icy fingers.

I pull my foot away. "Why did you ask me what the matter was, if you knew?"

My mother disposes of my question with a frown. "The important thing is that she's willing to change your grade. You just have to get the papers done."

"What makes you think I'll do any better on them?"

"Look, there's been a misunderstanding. She'll look at your papers differently now. You'll just have to do your best work."

I raise my book in front of my face.

"But you have to get going. Listen to me, Rachel, you don't want to ruin your record at this point!"

I stare at my book. My silence is a solid seamless wall which she can't penetrate.

She hesitates, then stands up abruptly. "I don't know what's going on with you, Rachel. I can't talk to you anymore!" She slams my bedroom door as she leaves.

I lock it and turn up my radio. Laura Branigan's voice comes whirling at me. ". . . I think you're headed for a breakdown, so careful not to show it. You really don't remember, was it something that he said? Or the voices in your head, calling Gloria?" One voice too many. I switch it off. All those voices in my head. Mr. Reese's, my mother's, Mrs. Baker's.

Reese: You have promise. Mrs. Baker: You promise nothing. Mother: You know what Mrs. Baker said is not true.

I go over to my desk and take out my story. I'll make it not true. I flip open the book. What was I going to say next? I'll take it a step at a time.

"Karen picked up the phone and dialed quickly.

"'Hello?' The voice was deep, a little impatient.

"She could still hang up. She was still safe. But she cleared her throat. 'Hi, Michael. It's Karen.'

"'Oh, hi, Karen. What can I do for you?'

"Cold. Distant. As though she was a nuisance, a pest. 'I was just wondering if you'd heard about Amanda's party tonight. I didn't know if she'd had a chance to call, and I just wanted to let you know . . .' She was letting him know, all right. She was telling him everything. She felt as transparent as—"

As what? What's the image I need to capture that stripped, exposed feeling? What was it Mrs. Baker said, that I wasn't precise enough? Where's the phrase that will prove her wrong? But my head is all fuzziness and words that skitter away.

I put down my pencil, seeing Mrs. Baker's faint, knowing smile. Next to me is my notebook containing our latest English assignment, a paper on madness in King Lear that's due tomorrow—a paper I haven't even started. All right, Mrs. Baker, you win. But I have my weapons too.

After dinner, I take up my post at my desk. Eight o'clock. Three hours till eleven. Three hours in which to do my paper. Here my mother is all concerned over my two extra papers, when only tomorrow I have a sterling opportunity to win one of those coveted A's.

I open my math book, losing myself in its clear, contained demands. Every once in a while I glance up curiously at the clock. Forty-five minutes pass. I wonder if I feel worried. No, only a kind of interested distance, as I watch myself move slowly toward some forbidden point.

At ten o'clock I close my books. There. It's almost done. I'll watch television for an hour and go to bed.

"What have you been doing all this time?" my mother calls out as I pass the living room.

"Homework. What else?"

"Oh." Uncertainty. Fire temporarily held. Homework could include those extra papers, after all.

Let her think that. Let her worry about them, while I earn the family its first F.

chapter 10

I hover in the mouth of the alley, my cave, my hide-
away. I watch while Susan and Terry give up on me,
while they walk toward the bus stop. While the bus
slides past the end of the street, its rumble stretching
thin in the distance.

Then I step out onto the sidewalk and start walking. I
have no idea what I'm going to do. I cross to the bus stop
and wait.

In about fifteen minutes, another bus arrives. I climb
on and take a window seat. Empty except for some elderly people and a few parents with young children. We
pass a little girl in a pink jacket pushing a plastic lawn-
mower in her front yard. A Pekingese about two inches
high barks ferociously at the bus. I lean back peacefully.
I'll be at least fifteen minutes late for school.

The bus pulls up at the sprawling red building. The school looks quiet, all its activity tucked inside. I make no move to get up. As the bus pulls away, I feel as though I've passed to the other side of something. I'm Alice, stepping through the looking glass. Columbus, sailing to new worlds. I feel so giddy. I'm getting a little carsick.

Between the passing houses, I see the water of the Sound, bits of blue satin against coarser burlap. At Julie's stop, I ring the bell and get off. As I slip down the access path to the beach, I examine myself for incipient madness. All I need is one of Mrs. Danby's children to pipe up with, "There's Julie's friend!"

I hurry along the rocks, crouching low, but no hand clutches my collar; no voice trumpets my wrongdoing. There is only the distant cry of gulls over the rhythmic swish of the water.

What am I doing here at nine-thirty on a Friday morning? Homeroom has already passed, as well as part of math. The precise words for what I'm doing, Mrs. Baker, are playing hooky.

Well, then play I will. I push my book bag behind me. If I keep my gaze fixed a little to the right, so that I can't see the shore, I can pretend that the world doesn't exist. There is only me, the sliding silver-blue water, and the pale sky stroked with faint white clouds, like erasures.

I pick up a piece of straw and bend it between my fingers. The sun warms my face and sends its light onto the water in tiny dancing drops. A patch of white moves on the horizon. A sailboat. Sailed by a boy with a strong brown body. He draws near the shore, attracted by my siren call, my sultry good looks. I toss back my head, and stare at the horizon, as mysterious and brooding as Meryl Streep in *The French Lieutenant's Woman*. He can't take his eyes off me, but I give no sign that I am conscious of my allure. He sails his boat onto the shore and comes toward me across the rocks.

Something *is* coming across the rocks. I turn, Meryl Streep greeting Charles with her mesmerizing stare. But it's not a beautiful brown-skinned boy. It's a fat lady with a dog. A truant officer! I don't even know if there are truant officers anymore. But I have a strong inclination to run.

Instead, I turn to greet her. It's better to act unconcerned. She smiles and nods pleasantly. Her look is almost apologetic in its mildness. What is she apologizing for? Her size? Her little dachshund is almost as round as she is.

I glance at my watch. Ten o'clock. The beginning of English class. I sit up straighter. I have to be conscious of every moment of my resistance.

Mrs. Baker is collecting our papers. I watch as they are passed over my empty desk into her waiting hands. She puts them aside and begins to talk, orchestrating her words with small staccato movements. At first, she is all involved with the sweet harmonies of Shakespeare's song, but at some point during the class, she notices my absence. For an instant, she senses that it's deliberate.

I sit upright, watching the remainder of the class in

the water. When it's over, I lean back with a feeling of accomplishment. I look around for my sailboat. It's gone, vanished over the horizon. But my pangs are more of hunger than heartbreak. I open my lunch bag. The water foams around the rocks, trimming them with white lace. Its rustling skirts wrap around me. I could stay here all day. I *will* stay here all day. I'll go home only when I'm ready.

Small waves suddenly rush into the rocks at my feet. I watch them forming a pool before I realize what it means. Only a thin strip of rocks remains. The tide is coming in. I guess I won't be staying all day.

A bus passes as I come up from the beach, and I climb on. An old woman with bleached blonde hair and a drooping face is complaining about her landlord in a droning voice.

The bus climbs the bridge over the harbor, taking me to Oz, to Wonderland, to a new life. I get as far as the New Haven green and get up.

"Hey, girlie, you forgot your book." The lady shakes her head with disapproval as I grab the math book that slipped from my bag.

I cross the street to Yale's old campus, scene of my date with Damien on Tuesday, scene of my fiasco. Paint over the picture, erase the tape, record a new scene: daylight, boys and girls crossing the walks, packs on backs, long hair flowing. Two girls come toward me down the path. I smile, a chummy, haven't-I-seen-you-in-class-somewhere smile of equals.

"I don't know if I can make it. I have a paper and

89

geology lab . . ." the one in a quilted vest and madras skirt is saying as they pass. Matter-of-fact, comfortable, sure of her credentials. There's nothing equal about us.

Theodorus Dwight Woolsey, past president of these lofty edifaces, stares down at me with a disapproving stone face. I hurry out of the quadrangle and across the street. What in my misguided unconscious made me escape to this spot—the very center of academic endeavor, of academic pressure? I'll bet the halls are full of Mrs. Bakers. Only the warped mind of a professor's daughter could conceive of this as playing hooky.

A bearded man in a suit with a pack on his back approaches me. A professor, a throwback, a descendant of those scholarly medieval monks who used to dwell within just such high stone walls as these. I duck into an archway to escape—right into the cloistered heart of Gothicism. Turreted stone walls, leaded glass windows laced with stonework. The real McCoy. Except for the inhabitants. Adidas, leg warmers, feathered hair. I pass a girl and a boy on a bench. The girl has her head in the boy's lap, and he's going through her hair with familiar tenderness. He may be looking for lice for all I know, but his gesture reminds me of David. Is he sitting with some girl's head on his lap just now? A girl with long yellow hair, who's a whiz at textual analysis? I feel suddenly isolated in the warm sunshine.

A group of women and men are clustered together on the walk. Ah, a tour, a protection. With the instincts of a stray dog, I trot over, smiling benevolently, assuring the rest of the pack it will be delighted by my presence.

90

"Branford College was built in the 1920s," a girl with the streamlined face of a Borzoi is saying. "It was meant to be an exact replica of Gothic architecture. Even those niches in the walls are empty, since the statues would have been knocked out by invaders in medieval times." Knowing Yale, they probably put the statues in and then proceeded to knock them out, in the interests of authenticity. I stick with my adopted gang until I am safely out on the street. Then I resume my fickle, solitary way.

A boy hurries by, his jacket buttoned crooked, clutching an open book and talking to himself. I begin to feel more at home. Actually, I feel positively superior to that poor boy. It occurs to me that I'm probably the only one around who doesn't have to rush off to a class or an exam.

Two boys pass me as I go down the steps to the green. One gives me an approving smile. Red turtleneck, navy Windbreaker, small gold earrings accepted. The admissions office be damned.

Students crisscross the paths. A stocky, silver-haired man is walking with a pretty redhead. He is nodding, his gaze attentive, amused, admiring. I step back. What is my father doing here, in my Yale, in my escape? Is that the wonder woman from Wisconsin? A student of exceptional promise? I reach into my bag for my French book, opening it protectively in front of my face. I would probably have to be a Keynesian with a Marxist bent to interest my father that way.

They disappear around a building. A girl and boy

91

meet another boy on the steps in front of me. "Hi ya, Tony."

Tony puts his arm around the girl. She is pretty in a sharp-featured way.

"You smell sweet," she teases.

"It's just my sweet nature." The boy is tall and beefy. "How's it going? How about coming and studying with me? You'll just look into my eyes, and . . ."

"And read the answers to the history exam?" The girl laughs and turns to the other boy. "Joining us, Jim?"

"I'll see you later in the Commons." Jim could be the girl's brother, with his straight dark blond hair and slim figure. He looks at me, and I glance quickly away. Darn. Foiled. I love eavesdropping. I would happily stand smack in between two people and listen if I could remain undetected.

He comes over to me. I quickly raise my *Le Rouge et le Noir* and stare into it intently.

"Hi, there. Enjoying the spring weather?" Friendly, casual, at ease with himself.

"I always like spring when it comes in December." I keep my eyes with scholarly dedication on my book.

"You look pretty engrossed there. Have an exam?"

"Uh, no, just some papers to write." Has my nose grown larger, my tongue turned black? It's not a full-fledged lie. I didn't say what school they were for.

He glances at my book. "French papers?"

I shut it quickly. "No, English."

"English? For what course? I'm surprised I haven't seen you around before. I'm an English major."

"Oh, well, you see, I'm an economics major. I'm just taking this one Shakespeare course." Why did I choose economics? What I know could fit on a thumbnail.

"You must have Dr. Milner for Shakespeare. He's really quite a performer, isn't he?"

"Sure is." I pick up my bag. "Better get started on those papers."

"I was just heading down to Naples for a snack. How about taking a break and coming with me?" He bends toward me and smiles, all corn-silk graciousness.

This may be a little more acceptance than I bargained for. I don't know if I'm attracted to him. Too blond, smooth-edged, placid. Still, I don't want to turn down such an exclusive offer. I'm playing hooky, right? Who knows, maybe I'm about to discover one of those arty coffeehouses Damien was so avid for. "Okay, for a while."

We start walking across the green. "I'm Jim Malachowsky, by the way."

Malachowsky? He looks more like a Jim Brooks, or a Smith. "I'm Rachel. Rachel—" Rachel what? It could be that he's heard of my father. "—Rains."

"Rachel Rains? That's very alliterative."

"It is, isn't it?"

"And so you're an economics major? That's interesting. I'm pretty ignorant on the subject. What are you studying?"

"Oh, macroeconomics. Income maintenance with Professor Gilbert. All that stuff. And what about you?" I add quickly.

"Oh, my field is Victorian Literature. Tennyson and Browning, and those fellows."

Right. Of course. Those fellows. Just the guys next door, the gang on the block. Is that what Yale's erudite English department does? Puts you on a first name basis with the greats?

"Ah, here we are." An expert arm steers me through the door of Naples as I am about to walk blithely by.

I obviously have yet to visit an arty coffee shop. Naples seems to be a rather plain pizza and sandwich place.

"My favorite is their meatball sub. What's your usual?"

My usual? I look up at the items listed above the counter with nearsighted bleariness. Someone walks by with a pizza. "Oh, pizza is what I usually get."

"Right. But that's over there at that other counter."

"Oh, of course." I move to the other counter and order some pizza and a Coke. They must still drink Coke at Yale. I wonder if we're supposed to go dutch. I didn't leave the house this morning prepared for an outing at Naples.

"I'll pay for hers." Jim comes up next to me. "We can sit over here." He leads us to a booth in a small room occupied by other student-looking types. I try to walk gracefully, as though I balance a pizza and a Coke and my books every day. I have discovered at least one break in my camouflage, one false note in my impersonation. Book bags are out and backpacks are in. I surreptitiously slide the offending item to the end of the seat and cover it with my jacket. I see Jim looking approvingly at my red sweater.

"So, Rachel Rains, where do you come from? I'm still surprised I haven't seen you around before. You must be a junior at least, if you're majoring already."

"Oh, well, no. I didn't mean I was actually majoring. Just sort of getting a head start on some of my courses." I lower my head in intense concentration on my pizza.

"Which college are you in?"

Inventing familiarity with a college is more than I can handle. "I don't live here. I live at home."

"Home? Where is that? New Haven?"

"No, West Gate. It isn't far."

"Well, I'm in Trumbull this year."

"What's that like? I've never been in it."

"You haven't? We'll have to rectify that. As soon as we're done, I'll show you my room."

I start to eat my pizza at the rate of a hibernating bear. There's a limit to how long you can make a slice of pizza last, however, and in a short while we're out on the sidewalk again, headed back toward campus. Jim seems to assume I'm coming with him, and so I go, a piece of fluff on the wind, a sail waiting to be filled.

We step between the parked cars on High Street. "Watch it!" A girl in a beret is headed for me on a bicycle. Jim hauls me back by my jacket. "I can see you need some watching out for. High Street goes that way, remember?"

"Guess I looked the wrong way." How do I know

95

which blasted way High Street goes? I'm likely to sail into the wrong college. I walk a discreet half-step behind Jim, hoping he'll lead the way.

"Here we are." We turn under the stone archway to Trumbull. A girl and boy are hugging and kissing, dancing around like two bears in a clinch. I study the graceful arch of the ceiling intently as we pass.

Inside the courtyard, a girl in a black coat comes out of a doorway. "Hi, Jim." She has a square-jawed model's face. For a minute I feel ridiculously possessive.

Jim turns into the same door the girl came out of. "Gail's in the room across from us. We have a bathroom in common."

"Oh?" I lower my eyes, so as not to reveal my visions of towel-bedecked figures in awkward encounters.

"The girls have later classes, so we take it first. No problem."

So much for Phyllis Schlafly and the terrors of unisex bathrooms.

Jim goes up a curving staircase, past dark wooden doors. I'm Rapunzel, being led to the tower; Bluebeard's victim lured to his lair. I'm ready to fly back down the stairs.

He opens a door and I hold my breath. A brown canvas chair and a long table with a typewriter appear. At least it isn't a king-size bed and red plush carpeting.

It's a nice room, actually, with a leaded glass window all along one wall. A boy with a long rubbery body is draped across a beanbag chair in front of a small fire, reading some typed papers.

96

"Rudy, this young lady has yet to be introduced to the glories of Trumbull College."

"Then you've come to the right place. This is the deluxe suite of Trumbull, home of gracious living. Witness the raging fire, the rich wood paneling, the delicately carved gargoyles adorning the mantelpiece." Rudy swings his beer bottle in sweeping arcs. "And go and admire the masterly job of carpentry done in the bedroom by our friend Jim."

"Rudy, you're sloshed. Why don't you sit down, Rachel, and take off your jacket?"

I sit down on the couch, knocking into the stack of newspapers on the coffee table. The entire superstructure of papers and empty coffee mugs quakes. I reach out and grab the Sony Walkman tottering on top.

"Sorry, we didn't realize we'd be having company." Jim stands above me. "Want a beer?"

"Uh, no thanks. I just had a Coke." Rachel Rains, brilliant conversationalist.

"A little bit of beer makes the paperwork go down . . ." Rudy takes a drink from the bottle. "As well as decorates the room." He gestures toward the line of beer bottles on the mantelpiece.

"Say, Rudy. Rachel's in economics too. She's a student of Professor Gilbert. You two should know each other."

"Gilbert? How do you like him? I had a course with him last year. I liked his lectures better than his grades."

"Oh, he's okay." I try to imagine him at the front of a

97

class. I think of the girl on the green. "He's always available if you need to discuss something with him."

"I'm surprised I haven't seen you around."

"I haven't really taken a lot of economics courses yet. And I've been doing some independent work." So independent that I'm not even in the school.

"I wonder if your paper's here, in the ones I've been grading. You taking Economics II?"

"Not this semester." I get up quickly and go over to the bookcase next to the fireplace. What should I talk about? Marx? *Bullfinch's Mythology*? Why did I come up here? "Well, I better be going."

"But you haven't seen all the glories of Trumbull. What's your hurry?" Jim cocks his head at me and sticks his hands in his pockets.

"Speaking of hurry, that's what I'd better do. Have to get these papers in by three." Rudy scoops up a pile from the floor and deposits his beer bottle on a shelf. "Another job well done." He gives me a wide grin and scoots out the door.

I'm not sure that I feel his departure has lessened the danger.

"Let me show you our home in its entirety."

"Oh, that's all right. I get the general effect." I wave my hand vaguely.

"I'll tell you what. You can make a comparison of a Yale bedroom versus a Malachowsky bedroom."

"Why, how many bedrooms are there?" I walk to the doorway where Jim is standing. Maybe I should just act like a girl from across the hall being given a house tour.

98

"Two. There are four of us in here. Voilà. The idea is to give us more space underneath."

Two loft beds have been built at right angles to each other near the ceiling. What they seem to have given more room for is piles of clothes, which overflow from a closet whose door probably hasn't been closed in twenty years.

"They look pretty sturdy. That must have been some job." I feel more relaxed. You can't be thrown down on a bed that's up in the air.

"It just took a few days. I've done a lot of carpentry in my youth."

"I once made a lamp for my grandparents. It was the kind of thing only grandparents would love. It fell apart in three days." Is that a hand creeping up my back, or just something I'm leaning against?

Jim laughs. "I built a small boat at home. With boats and beds, it's kind of necessary that they stay together."

The hand has progressed to the back of my neck. How did I get this far into the room, anyway?

I turn and peer with deep interest at the Yale Film Society schedule on the wall. "Oh, they're having *The 400 Blows*. I've seen that on TV."

Jim has given up on my neck. He's nuzzling my cheek with his lips. "That was really a powerful movie, especially the—"

Jim takes my chin and turns my face toward him. He kisses me. Long and slow. Soft, beery smell. Tongue against my teeth, my tongue. Holding me there with his arm around my shoulder. It's nice. A little too nice. His arm slides down from my shoulder. My God, where's he going? His hand lands firmly on my rear. I can see why he built the beds up in the air. He doesn't need them.

I step back, staring hard at a tennis racket tossed on a pile of clothes, smoothing back my hair. How do I get out of this gracefully, without showing I'm petrified? How would the girl in the black coat handle it?

"Look—" I turn to Jim. He's gazing at me with amusement. "—I really do have to get to those papers."

"Sure." Jim steps aside. That was easy enough.

I retrieve my book bag from the couch. Jim gives me a light kiss on the cheek. "Nice meeting you, Rachel Rains."

It occurs to me that by giving him my alias, I've prevented him from getting in touch with me. I'm not sure how I feel about that. But I can't blow my cover now.

"Hope you get your papers done. Since it's reading period next week, I can see your concern. Papers were all due by today." He raises his eyebrows and grins at me. He knows! How long has he known?

"'Bye. Thanks for showing me Trumbull." I walk with elaborate dignity to the door.

chapter 11

"You look pleased about something." My mother glances up from the embroidered Mexican blouse she is ironing.

"Um-hmm." I snatch a banana from the counter.

"Have a good day in school?" She rests the iron on its end, ready to hear all about it.

I slowly peel the banana. "I had a good day because I wasn't in school."

"Was there a trip? You didn't tell me about it."

"No, there wasn't a trip. I just didn't go to school." I watch the news settle heavily on her forehead, drawing her eyebrows together.

"If you weren't in school, where were you?"

"Oh, on the beach for a while. And then I went to

New Haven. I spent this afternoon at Yale, as a matter of fact. You should approve of that."

"Rachel, you played hooky!" My mother's face tightens in a combination of disbelief and anger. She knows whom my action was directed against. "How could you do such a thing? What's happening to you?"

"For the first time in my life I wasn't just a good little girl doing what I was told. I did what I wanted, and it felt great!"

"It won't feel so great if you get expelled from school!"

"The school doesn't have to know anything about it."

"What do you mean?" But my mother knows. An angry red heats her cheeks.

"You're so good at writing notes, Mom. All you have to do is write one saying I was home sick, and the school won't think another thing about it." I turn and walk out, leaving my mother standing there.

I'm not worried. My mother isn't about to allow today to mar her daughter's unblemished record.

"I see that you were absent from school on Friday, Rachel." Mrs. Baker stares at me with wide sea-gray eyes.

"Yes." That's all you get, Mrs. Baker. No explanation. No note. No pleas. My only excuse went straight to the office this morning.

"Do you have your paper ready for me today, then?"

"No." Guilty, as accused. I await my sentence.

Mrs. Baker bites her lower lip. "You know what this

102

means, don't you, Rachel? I can't give you anything but an F for an undelivered paper."

I nod at her.

"Haven't you even started one? Maybe if you could show me what you've done, I could mark you on that. It would be better than nothing."

Poor Mrs. Baker. It's probably the first F she's handed out. I feel as though I should be reassuring her: It's all right. It won't kill me. I'll survive. Besides, you should get used to giving F's. Consider this a learning experience.

"I'm sorry, Mrs. Baker. I don't have anything to show you."

"I see." She looks slapped, defeated. Her head droops on her pipe cleaner-thin neck. I wait for her to straighten up again, but she stays bowed, in communion with herself. It seems I've been dismissed.

Damien is waiting for me in the hall. "Rachel, the galleys are back. We need a heading for our Daniels interview."

I station myself a few feet away, far enough not to sense his body. I look beyond him down the hall. The only way I know to make the other night not exist is to make Damien not exist.

"Can't now. I have an appointment with Mr. Reese. Why don't you write the headline? Mrs. Baker thinks you have such a gift for colorful phrases, I'm sure you'll think up something catchy."

Damien shrugs. "Sure." He turns and walks away with long, unhurried steps.

I stand there. What, no urging, no arguing, no flicking of hair? You give me up so easily, Damien? The hall seems hushed, bare, as though the tide had suddenly receded. Tides are supposed to be constant, steady, Damien. Not permanently withdrawn.

"Doctors and teachers always protect their own kind."

Julie looks at me with a grin. "You sound bitter."

"Oh, I just had a conference with Reese."

"What happened? He didn't like what you'd written?"

"No, he stuck up for Mrs. Baker. Defended her good old one-track approach to literature. Said it has merit."

"Well, what did you expect?"

"I expected the truth." I expected a cohort, an ally who would decry the narrowness of the enemy's approach, the rightness of my stand against it. Instead, what I got was a shove into the enemy camp, a short, "Maybe you just need a little more practice with the technique." He was on *her* side.

"Oh, Julie, there you are." Mrs. Daniels's flat black gaze comes into sharp focus on Julie. "I was wondering if you could help me set up an experiment with hermit crabs for my tenth graders." She smiles, glows. Mrs. Daniels and Mrs. Baker, the twin lamps of West Gate High. I step back against the lockers.

"Sounds great. When do you need me?"

"Right now would be good, if I'm not cutting into your lunch period."

"No, it's fine. I'll be right there." Julie comes over to me.

"How does it feel to be such a little protégé?" Gilbert's punishment for desertion. But I need Julie as much as Mrs. Daniels does.

"Come on, Rachel. We'll talk later. Want to get together after school?"

"Okay, if it's your place. My mother's getting on my nerves."

"Your mother? About what? Did you have a fight?"

"In a way." I shrug. Suddenly I want Julie to hear the worst about me, to tell me it's all right, that I'm all right. "My mother wrote a note to Mrs. Baker."

"A note? What about?"

"She told Mrs. Baker that she wasn't grading me fairly."

"Oh, terrific. Did you know she was doing it?"

I nod.

Face frozen. Mouth slightly twisted in distaste, as though I had confessed to cheating, or shoplifting, or passing counterfeit bills. "Why didn't you stop her?"

How can I explain why I accepted the note? Julie has never asked for special treatment in her life.

"Well." Her face relaxes. "You probably couldn't stop her anyway, if she was set on it. Mrs. Baker won't blame you."

Stop it? I didn't dream of stopping it. I was happy for

it; I wanted it in Mrs. Baker's hands as much as you want your chance to study crustaceans and mollusks.

I feel like that boy in *The 400 Blows,* an outcast from his family, from society, from his world. An outcast from myself. What I need is a built-in oyster's mantle to regrow my defective parts.

chapter 12

Rachel, the thing is, these won't fit!" Robby tries to jam Peter's square foot into size one sneakers with all the might of his skinny arm.

"You can't do it by force, Robby. Measure his foot with a ruler. He needs something larger. Yes, what is it, Katie?"

"I don't want to sell these baby shoes. There's only one pair, so it looks silly!" Lower lip stuck out, braids tossed back. A regular Pippi Longstocking.

"Well, then put them away. But what will you do if a baby comes in the store? What's wrong, Felice?"

"Lucretia doesn't want her new shoes!"

"Then give her her money back. No, no, don't throw her shoes at her. Put them on her. Stuart and Linda, don't fight over that shoe polish. Take turns. Robby, Peter's boots are on backwards."

Robby is unconcerned. "Where's your money?" He grabs the piece of blue paper out of Peter's hand. "'Bye." Fastest sale I've ever seen. Robby certainly went for something larger. It looks like two-thirds of the boot is empty. Peter walks as if each step were in squishy mud.

I sit back on my heels in relief. As soon as Julie and I walked in today, Mrs. Danby requisitioned us. Her assistant was sick, and we were handy replacements. So now I am managing a shoe store run by three and four year olds, and Julie, a portrait in boredom, is helping the little two year olds build with blocks. She's sitting cross-legged, her chin resting on her hand, releasing each block like a poison pellet. Mrs. Danby, general manager of chaos, is in the living room reading a poem to some of the customers from the store. " . . . Bright shoes, white shoes, dandy-dance-by-night shoes . . ."

"Rachel, your husband is on the phone." Stuart is sitting behind the cashier's box, holding a wooden receiver toward me.

"Tell him I'll call back. I'm busy now."

"She's very busy, so hang up and don't call again," Stuart says in his deep little man's voice, and slams down the phone. "Oops, Rachel, he just called back."

I take the receiver. "No, Horace, I'm not buying any more shoes today."

"Rachel, I'm upset!"

108

"'Bye, Horace, got to run. I've got a disgruntled sales-lady. What's the matter, Felice?"

"People keep coming into my department and bothering me."

"Well, those shoes are for everyone, Felice. It's really okay to share. What are those papers in the slippers?" She's stuck white pieces of paper with wavy red lines in each shoe.

"Bumblebees."

"Bumblebee shoes, or real bumblebees?"

"Rachel, your husband just called back."

"Tell him I'm busy."

"Real bumblebees, the stinging kind."

"He won't hang up. He wants to know what you're having for dinner."

"You might lose some customers that way, Felice. Horace, we're having gumbo soup, now please—"

"Oh, my goodness." A little girl with a bowl of blond hair is standing in the doorway, staring at the shoes.

"Got to hang up, Horace. A new customer needs to be shown around." I take the child's soft, buttery hand. "Robby, my daughter needs some shoes. Can you help her?"

"Nope, not my department." Hands jammed into pockets, nose stuck into the air.

"Carolyn, can you help my daughter?" I ask a little girl with curly black hair and round kissable cheeks. She nods, and outfits my daughter in a pair of shiny red patent leather heels. My daughter beams. The sign of a good saleslady is knowing what the customer wants.

"Rachel, your husband's on the phone again."

"What does he want this time?"

"P.U., he stinks!" A little girl is pointing at the toddler seated next to Julie, happily knocking down the blocks Julie has set up. Julie is leaning back with alarm.

"Jason needs his diaper changed, Julie." Mrs. Danby starts across the room. "If you take over for me, I'll do it. We're talking about the different shoes we're all wearing."

"Rachel, your husband wants to order some black and white shoes."

I reach for the phone. "Horace, I don't think we have them in your size."

"Jen, I feel sick!" Poor Peter. I hope it wasn't his experience in the shoe store.

"Hold on, Peter, I'll get you upstairs to the bathroom." Mrs. Danby runs Peter up the stairs with more speed than I thought her capable of. Nonemergencies like diaper changes are forgotten.

"P.U., he smells." Several other children take up the chant. Julie looks at me helplessly.

"Good-bye, Horace. Be right back, kids." I don't know why I've suddenly become Florence Nightingale. I've never changed a diaper in my life.

With the helpful memory of some TV commercials, I proceed. Actually, except for the pungent odor, the experience is less harrowing than I expected. Jason relaxes amiably on the floor. I apply Wet Ones liberally to his

110

bottom and fasten a Pamper over his round belly. There is something satisfyingly complete about pulling the child's pants up over the fresh diaper and sending him on his way.

Mrs. Danby returns from her upstairs duty. "Peter's resting. How's the shoe store going?" I follow her back to the commercial district. The dining room looks like it's been spun around in a clothes dryer. "I think it's time to do some straightening up. Salespeople, have you told your customers about the free feely sidewalk outside? They can do that while you're cleaning up. Just take off your shoes and see what it feels like."

The customers stream into the living room and start running over the pieces of carpet and cardboard and plastic Mrs. Danby has laid down.

Carolyn is carefully arranging ladies' shoes along her section of the dining room table. I sit down in a chair against the wall. "Hello, Miss. I need some new high heels. What can you show me?"

A shy, pleased smile. Small, gentle hands untie my sneakers. She turns to the table and plucks down a pair of sparkly white heels with rhinestone buckles, carrying them as though she sees a world in them.

"Those are very pretty. And look at those beautiful buckles." I am a most amiable customer.

"They're real diamonds."

She holds out a shoe. I push, I squeeze, I huff. I'm a wicked stepsister trying to fit into the glass slipper, the large, grown-up girl trying to jam herself back into her childhood dreams. I look up at the disappointed little

111

face. "My feet must be a little swollen today. But I think the shoes are lovely. I'll take them."

Smiles. Dimples. It's so direct, so satisfying, pleasing a child. Not all tied up with other things. Just there.

I receive the precious shoes, neatly boxed, for which I am charged an exorbitant five pieces of blue paper.

"All right, everyone, it's time to put on your shoes and your coats. Your parents will be here in five minutes," Jen announces.

In the general scramble, Julie grabs me and heads for the stairs.

"Don't you think we should help your aunt?"

"Let's get out while we can." Julie locks her bedroom door behind us and looks quickly around her room. "What a way to spend an afternoon. Next time you come over, we check on the health of Jen's assistant first!" She takes off her jacket for the first time since we've been home.

I start to agree. But then I realize, weirdo that I am, that I liked the afternoon. I liked my husband Horace, and the bumblebees, and my Cinderella slippers. I liked those funny, serious voices, those direct little personalities. Most of all, I liked being so busy that I forgot about Rachel Gilbert.

chapter 13

It's dark as I walk up the street to my house. A ripple of snow shines under the lamplight. Winter has finally come. I bend down and stick my fingers into the smooth pits the rain drilled in the crusty surface, like Carolyn might, or Robbie—testing, tasting, describing. My head is full of their small voices.

I've been at Mrs. Danby's almost every day after school for the past two weeks. Even though her assistant has returned. Even though Julie has made it her business to be there as little as possible. But it is not Julie I go for.

My house has a strange, hollow feel. The living room is empty, and there are no sounds coming from the kitchen. I once saw a comedy show on TV about a boy's parents running away from home because he was so boring. Maybe my parents have deserted me because I'm so unsatisfactory. I want to call out into the stillness, but I don't. I go down the hall to my bedroom.

My mother is standing over my desk. Her face is thin with anger. "Rachel, you haven't even started on these applications! And it's practically the deadline!"

"I know." I know it's December seventeenth. I know it's fourteen days until the end of the month, two weeks to the day to get my applications done. A fortnight, as dear old Shakespeare would say. I shrug.

"Don't you realize what will happen to you if you don't get them done? There'll be no place for you."

"There's no place for me now."

"What is that supposed to mean? Rachel, how can you ruin everything you've been working for? Everything I've been working for? What's wrong with my children?" My mother stares at my desk, as though asking it her question. "I put all my energies into them, do everything I can think of for them, and they end up turning their backs on it all. What do you think I've been working for these last few years?" My mother whips around toward me, the skin tight over her face. "For myself? Do you think I find great pleasure spending my days in that building? I do it so that my daughter can have the pick of any school in the country. And this is how you thank me!"

Ingratitude, thou marble-hearted fiend . . . I gaze into the Alpine snow scene on my shelf. Under my mother's glare, I'm shrinking to the size of the little red and green

114

people on the mountain slope. I'll climb in there with them, shake up the snow in great cushioning swirls . . .

"If you weren't spending all your time with Julie, you would have a much better chance of getting them done!"

I look at my mother. "I haven't been with Julie, Mother. I've been helping Mrs. Danby with her day-care children."

"Why in the world would you want to do that?"

"Because I like it. Because I enjoy the children." Because the weighty question of where Rachel Gilbert will go to college doesn't enter those walls. Other things matter, other skills I didn't even know I had. "Who knows? Maybe I'll end up a nursery school teacher."

"You wouldn't want to do a thing like that, Rachel!" Here she is forced to spend her days in a child's world when it's the last place she wants to be, and I turn around and choose it. Her face is painted bright pink. What color would she turn if I said I wanted to be a pusher, or a prostitute?

"You're much too smart for that."

Smart? Mrs. Danby isn't smart when she has the children imagine a snail's world, when she teaches a child not to be afraid of the hamster by putting him in charge of feeding it? "Maybe I'm not so smart! Maybe Mrs. Baker is right about me."

"Don't be silly, Rachel. Of course you're smart. It's just that women have always had the low-paying, low-prestige jobs. I don't want you to settle for that. You have to aim higher."

115

"Just like you've done? You give up on yourself, and then you expect me to do everything you haven't. You can't have your career through me!"

I stand there, expecting my mother to slap me. But she just looks at me with a sort of collapsed expression. "Is that the way you feel, that I'm living through you?" Her hands raise and then drop. She sits on the bed, but I remain standing, a negotiating distance away.

"It's just that I don't want you to do what I've done, Rachel. I suppose I've always accepted the way life has pushed me without resisting. When my parents needed more money to send my younger brother to college, I said okay and left school. When I married your father, I used the money I had saved to go back to school to help put him through graduate school. I want you to have your chance before circumstances close in on you."

"But that doesn't explain why you gave up painting. Nobody made you." I stand above her, unrelenting, unforgiving.

My mother looks down at her long slender fingers. "No, I suppose not. I guess I was afraid. I was never willing to take the instruction and to risk the effort of trying to be really good. So of course I had nothing to put up against the need for earning some money. And after I went back to work, it became difficult to find the time, and I just let it slide . . ."

That's what I was afraid of. I look out the window, away from my mother's stooped figure. Her defeat seems to have entered me, solid, cold, and heavy. Maybe that's all there is, a kind of shrinking. Maybe it's not possible

116

to stretch yourself, to dream of putting your words down on paper . . . I turn suddenly toward my mother.

"But that was a long time ago. Now that you see it, you can do something about it. You can look for something you really want to do. Like Susan's mother. She didn't have any college and she started last year. You could go back now. You could take art courses and start painting again." I hear my voice rise, pushing against my mother.

For a moment, my words balance in the air, their possibility hovering around us. Then my mother hunches her shoulders. "I'm too old for that, Rachel. It's too late for me." She leans toward me. "I'm telling you all this for your sake, so you'll know not to make the mistakes I have."

I feel like all the windows in the house have slammed shut. My mother reaches out for me, but I rush past her into the bathroom, locking the door. I sit on the floor, putting my head on the hard toilet seat. "It's not like that. There are possibilities! There are!"

chapter 14

S quawk, squawk!" There is no doubt from whose scrawny throat the cries arise. Terry is flapping her bony, orange-sweatered arms.

"Oink, oink." Rick pinches his nose and adds his own dulcet tones. Moos and neighs and bleats pop up around the room. A veritable modern symphony, a zoologist's dream. A teacher's nightmare. I laugh.

Mrs. Baker is swamped, overwhelmed, inundated. She doesn't know how to dam the torrent. Her high forehead floods with red along the roots of her hair as she bends over her book. "Everybody please turn to page sixty-eight."

The barnyard quiets. Hands start flipping pages. How to get a class under your control: three little words,

"Turn to page . . ." We've been trained since age six. It's as good as pushing a button in our heads.

"Shakespeare uses animals as a contrast with the state of man in the play. On seeing Edgar in rags, Lear says, *unaccommodated man is no more but such a poor, bare, forked animal as thou art.* Man is reduced to the level of animals." Mrs. Baker looks up. She presses her advantage. "Who can give me some other examples of animal imagery? Marjorie?"

Ah, the weakest link, the path of least resistance. Clever, Mrs. Baker.

Marjorie pants through her open mouth as she flips over pages. "Oh, here, page thirty. Lear says, *thy wolvish visage* when he talks to Goneril." She looks up hesitantly.

"Yes, the wicked daughters are often compared to animals in the play. Who can give me some more?"

"Here, here, just the page before." If Cynthia stretches her arm out any more, she's going to topple over. The leaning tower of academic eagerness. "Lear says, *How sharper than a serpent's tooth it is / To have a thankless child.*"

"Shakespeare captures the pain Lear is feeling in one vivid image, doesn't he? All right, and what else?"

What else? Let's count the wolf images, the dog images. How many serpents to a scene? So what? I raise my hand.

"Yes, Rachel?" No time lag these days. The glance hops right to me. There's been a shift in the power structure, you see. Now Mrs. Baker wants something from me too.

"I don't see why we're studying animal imagery at all. I think it's nit-picking." I can't believe I said that. I sound like Terry.

All heads snap around, Rockettes on cue. There's complete silence, the hush before the storm. I feel like my Uncle Dan when a bear grabbed a tobacco pouch out of his pocket and he grabbed it back, right from the bear's teeth. Then he began to shake. Well, I've just started to shake.

Mrs. Baker looks white. She's standing very straight. "Just what do you mean, Rachel? Please explain yourself."

"I don't think it helps us understand the play any better. Shakespeare didn't expect us to sit here and dig out all the dog images and tiger images. He expected people to go see the play and hear the characters speak and watch Lear's descent into madness. That's why he wrote the play."

"That's perfectly true. But what we're doing is trying to look under the surface to see what went into his writing, what its ingredients are. It can only help us to understand the play in greater depth." Mrs. Baker's limp ponytail is doing a fast jig around her head.

"I disagree. The depth of the play comes from understanding Lear's rage and feelings of betrayal. It's the emotions and themes and characters that count. The language is their vehicle."

"Of course. That's why I'm dealing with the lan-

120

guage. If you see its patterns and designs, then you can understand the themes of the play better. I'm putting the language at the service of the characters."

"No, you're not. You're taking it away from them! You're making the language a two-dimensional puzzle!"

Mrs. Baker's head jerks as though I've reached behind her and yanked her ponytail. Her eyes slip beyond me to the wall. What is she seeing? The small Gainsborough landscape prints she has hung like icons? Me, hung in effigy? As she stands there, she has the audacity to start to smile. You don't smile in the middle of a battle, Mrs. Baker, especially when you're losing.

"Rachel, do you enjoy art and music? What I mean is, do you go to many concerts or art museums?"

"Museums, sometimes." What is this, an attack from a new direction? Show your opponent to be a cultural ignoramus, and you discredit her right to judge? I should have known you'd be underhanded, Mrs. Baker. I should have known you'd bring it all back to the basic incompetence of Rachel Gilbert.

"Please do this for me. Take any painting you want, one you have a print of, and do a two-page paper on it. Put down anything you see in it about the colors, the patterns, use of light—anything. Bring it to me after Christmas vacation. All right, class, let's go on with the imagery."

Fie on thy wolvish visage, Mrs. Baker! Is that all my protest earns me, an extra paper? Like Cordelia, I get nothing? You have about as much sense of fairness as Lear.

121

"Good work, Rachel. You really gave it to Mrs. Baker." Terry clutches my arm in the hall. Her small green eyes are wide, and her mouth curves in true delight.

She has discovered a compatriot, a countryman among foreigners. True, from an unexpected direction, but so much the better. She has realized, you see, that I speak her language, the language she shares with her mother.

"A lot of good it did." I start walking up the hall.

"You just have to keep at it, that's all. Keep hammering away. Between the two of us we should be able to take Miss Highbrow down a peg or two. We'll break her self-righteous back!"

Is that what I want, to make Mrs. Baker bend? To deflate her literary ego? I don't know. Whatever it is, Terry is overestimating my power. It occurs to me that Mrs. Baker handled me better than any other challenge she's had so far.

"Wait up, Rachel!" Julie hurries toward us, her light hair flapping like small wings.

"My, my. You look all excited, Julie. I know! You've found the Loch Ness monster at last." Terry returns to her mother tongue.

"I haven't been to Scotland lately," Julie says quietly.

"Cut it out, Terry. Let her alone."

The green eyes flit between us, the forked tongue poised. Then she shrugs and turns away. Do snakes shrug? Well, anyway, I've acquired a new expertise to list on my applications: snake charmer.

"Guess what, Rachel?" Ten-gallon smile. Eyes the color of the Sound on a sunny day. Terry was right. Something big is up.

122

"You did find the Loch Ness monster."

"Better. You know how I've been helping out Mrs. Daniels? Well, she's been talking to me about what I'm going to do next year. Today she actually offered to help send me to the University of Miami!"

"She did?" Voice surprised, properly pleased. No sign of the green spiral of jealousy rising in my chest.

"She said that her husband left her with enough money so that she really doesn't have to work, and that her only daughter makes a good income herself. She said that there was nothing better she could do with her money than to use it to help someone she thought would eventually do good work in biology."

I force myself to turn my ungenerous gaze on my friend. "And what are you going to do? Are you going to take it?"

Julie nods slowly. "I think I will. I think she meant it genuinely. Oh, I wouldn't take it all from her, but with the money I've saved, and maybe a student loan, and a bit of Aunt Jen's money, I could make it through next year, at least. And then I could see."

"You should take it. You deserve it." I'm glad she's grabbing the opportunity. I'm not big on hugging, but I touch her arm. "I'm happy for you."

As we walk down the hall, I can't help making small-minded comparisons. No teacher has shown that kind of interest in me, and why should they? No burning desires, no special mark upon the brow. Nothing to set me apart from the hordes of bright students working their diligent way through high schools across the land. Nothing burning, except my need.

chapter 15

It is Sunday morning, the day after Christmas, and my mother and I are traveling around the house as if attached to opposite ends of a string. I hold the ladder for my father while he cleans out a gutter, and my mother stands frowning at me through the window. I go into the den for Scotch tape, and she watches me from the couch. I fill the bird feeders outside, and she follows me from room to room. Only when I stay in my own room, in close proximity to my applications, does the string slacken.

I'm happy in my room, reading comfortably on my bed, contentedly ignoring the solid white desk and all its serious contents. The thick applications on top. The notebook, where I should be pinpointing, defining, dissecting, slicing, and analyzing Shakespeare, or discussing the patterns, colors, and other basic vocabulary of a painting. My composition book closed in a drawer.

It's not that I'm ignoring my writing; I just can't do it. I'm stuck. Blocked. Paralyzed. When I've tried to write something, my mind skips to that perfect, complete story that Mr. Reese expects of me. That I expect of me. I can't allow myself the mistakes, the fumblings, the tentative phrases that will get me on my way. Who says it's the means that's important? The end is everything.

I should have made an appointment with Mr. Reese before now. But I have nothing to show. A writer without writing is like a day without sunshine . . .

I look down at my book. *War and Peace.* This is my second reading. Of *Peace* anyway. I tended to skip over *War.*

There's a knock on my door, and my mother peers in. She looks tired. It's difficult, having a daughter like me. My brother Bobby called yesterday, on Christmas. I could tell from the way she talked to him that she misses him more, now that I've become so disappointing.

She looks at me and throws up her hands. "What in the world are you doing just lying there? You don't have time for that."

"I'm reading."

"Don't you realize that Friday is absolutely the latest you can send the applications out? You have to spend every minute of your vacation on them!"

"Just let me finish this chapter."

"No! Put down that book!" My mother grabs it out of my hands and tosses it behind her.

125

You can't throw Tolstoy on the floor! My fingers tingle with the shock. "What are you getting so excited about?"

"Get up this instant!" My mother yanks my arm. She has never tried to force me to do something before, and her violence frightens me. But through my astonishment, I also have the desire to laugh. We must make a ridiculous sight, my mother tugging and jerking my arm, her earrings swinging furiously, while my arm flops like a dying fish and my body lies stone still. I get up, not so much to satisfy her, as to change my picture of the scene.

She tries to push me over to my desk. "Stop that!" I stand with my legs apart, immovable. A face-off, with me as the puck. My mother switches from the physical to the verbal, an approach she's more familiar with.

"Rachel, get over to that desk! I'm going to stand here until you start working."

I stay rooted another minute. Then I shrug and go sit down. Sure, I'll fill them out. But it won't do you any good. Not with the holes in my record appearing faster than you can stuff them with notes.

I can hear my mother breathing heavily next to me. Maybe I should write about this. Pantings, pushings, orders, and angry voices—the true story of how applications get completed. I could send it in as a sample of my writing, something they urge you to do. Well, I must not be completely dried up. I seem to be writing in my head, if not on paper.

I pull out an application. From Brown University. I

start filling in all the simple facts. Clubs, societies, hobbies.

For the rest of the day and all of Monday I sit at my desk, doing what my mother wants. By bedtime Monday I have entered all the pertinent, fascinating, desirable details about myself that I can muster up for five applications. The only thing I haven't done are the essays. I feel dizzy just looking at them. They will not only reveal more about me as a person, but as the one thing I claim I want to be—a writer.

On Tuesday morning, I try again. "Tell us more about the people, places or institutions contributing to your personal development," the Princeton application urges. What people could be blamed for my development? Mr. Reese? He hasn't gotten very far with me. Mrs. Danby? My primary contributor of recent weeks. What places? Her day care.

"How are you doing, Rachel?" My mother comes over to the desk. "You're working on the essays? That's marvelous."

She backs off. The bed creaks under her. "How much have you done?"

"Only the one I'm working on."

"Well, you still have almost four days. That should give you enough time to get the rest done."

"Mmm."

"Then all you'll have to worry about is the two papers for Mrs. Baker. When you get those done, everything will be all right again. I'm sure you'll be tremendously relieved." My mother's voice flutes her joy. "Just let me know if there's anything I can get you."

She practically tiptoes out of the room. Then the footsteps pause, come back toward me. "May I see?" She leans over my shoulder. Face smoothed out, fresh, crisp. Until she starts reading. "Rachel, you can't send in this essay."

"Why not?"

"Because it's not suitable. They aren't interested in a little neighborhood day-care center. They're looking for more unusual experiences, like visiting China, or even working with a professor on a book, like Julie."

I look away. "I've never been to China."

"I don't mean that specifically. And I'm not saying your essay isn't interesting; it is. Just not for this. You've got to make them impressed with you."

"I've nothing to impress them with." I put down my pencil and get up.

"Sure you do. Tell them about your trip to France. Or the influence of Yale on your life. After all, we are connected to the University."

"It hasn't had any effect on my life." I walk toward the door.

"Rachel, where are you going?"

"To Mrs. Danby. To help out in her uninteresting little day-care center."

"What are you talking about? You have to stay here and finish your applications."

"I don't have to do anything."

"I forbid you to go!" My mother's face is as clenched as her fist on the doorknob.

"I'm going, Mom."

"Rachel!" Her eyes grab at me.

I walk past and pull my jacket out of the hall closet. Then I hurry out the door, letting it slam.

"You walked into a busy morning, Rachel. But then, they're all busy." Jen slabs peanut butter onto healthy whole wheat bread, and I follow up with the jelly.

"No problem. As a matter of fact, I like it. It makes me forget about—things."

She looks at me. "Things?"

"College. My parents want only the best for me."

"That's not so uncommon for parents."

"Not everybody has to go to college to do all right."

"No, but it helps. Don't use me as an example. I just happened to find this to do, and I like it. But I'm not in your position, with the opportunities you have. I'm not you. You have to decide what you want."

What I want. It's all up to me. Well, what I want is to stop being pushed, tugged. To just plain be left alone to rot if I want to!

Jen smiles at me. "It's hard for parents, you know. They can't help wanting things for their children. For instance, I worry about Julie being so isolated. Oh, she has some friends—you, and Tara, from our old neighborhood. But she's always going places by herself. Did she tell you about Hanover's? She has a job there selling

129

over Christmas vacation. I know she needs the money, but it takes up more time when she could be doing things with her schoolmates."

"But Julie likes being by herself. She doesn't go for large get-togethers."

"I know, but it seems to me that she carries it to an extreme. Tell me, Rachel, have you ever met her friend Tara?" Jen turns to me.

I shake my head.

"Well, isn't that a little unusual? Her two best friends? It's as though she can't deal with too many people at once."

I think of Julie in the lunchroom at school, making sure there are empty chairs between her and the other kids at the table. Julie sort of fades out of a conversation if there's more than one person around.

"And I wish she'd get herself a boyfriend. You have one, don't you, Rachel? I don't know why she hasn't dated; she's so pretty. Well, enough of my complaining. On with lunch."

On with lunch. On with life. On with nothing. I had a little boyfriend that went in and out with me, and what could be the use of it was more than he could see. . . . You're behind the times, Jen. I had a boyfriend. I had a lot of things. Now all I have is you. I follow her into the dining room with a tray full of plates.

The Sound races, tumbles, scurries toward shore on white crab claws. Small voices pipe up from the yard around me, demanding, asking, leaving no room for other thoughts, no room for me. I've stepped into a large protective box and left my baggage outside.

"Hit me, hit me!" Robby stands astride the walk as Felice tricycles toward him. I leave them to negotiate their collision.

"Want some?" Carolyn sticks a bowl of wet sand under my nose.

"Umm, delicious. Maybe a little more salt. What is it?"

"Fly squash."

"Yuck!" Stuart holds his nose. "Squashed flies!"

"That's not what I said. I said fly squash. The flies aren't in it, they made it."

Logical, in its way. Not very appealing, but logical.

"Hi, there. Julie put you to work?" Damien is standing on the steps to the beach, looking over the fence at me.

With his dark hair blowing around his sharp-boned face, he looks a little wild, like the rough gray rocks. An intruder. A messenger from the evil world. "No. Mrs. Danby has." I don't go over to the fence.

"You doing it for love or money?"

I grin. "For love, I guess."

The word attracts the children like honey. "Is that your boyfriend, Rachel?" Felice pedals up on her tricycle.

"No."

"Say,"—Damien smiles down at her—"have you ever seen a wild swan?"

131

The red ponytails rise like a propeller around her swiveling head. "Where? Where?"

Damien points down the beach. Two white swans are swimming toward us along the edge of the rocks. They move and yet are unmoving. If it weren't for their progress and an occasional arching of their necks, they would seem like white china figures on a glass pond.

The children spring to the fence. "Hey, look." "Are they real?"

"Sure they're real. They're looking for food."

"Can we feed them, Rachel?"

"Well, I guess so. Go get some bread from Jen."

The swans float in front of the house, peering at us with shiny black eyes. They obviously know when to expect a handout.

"Where do they come from?"

"The North Pole, silly."

Damien stoops down next to the children as they cast their bread upon the waters. "Well, you know where I think these swans might come from? From Long Island, right out there." He points across the Sound.

"How did they get here?"

"I think some people in big houses bought the swans for their ponds because they thought they were so pretty. But some of the swans didn't want to stay, and so they flew away and became wild." I'd forgotten how good Damien was with his brother.

"Or, there's something else they could be."

"What?"

"There's a story about ladies who have been turned into swans by an evil magician. All day they are swans,

132

but at night they turn back into women, and they dance until morning."

"Naw, they're swans. Look at their feet," Bobby points out. "That's just a story."

"It's true. They're ladies in feather dresses." Carolyn looks at Damien shyly.

"Where's their fingers?"

"What happens to their clothes?"

The swans move off, taking their mystery with them, and the children switch their attention to Damien, the next best thing. He answers their questions, focusing on each one with concentrated interest. The kind of interest I used to receive, the kind I seem to have permanently lost.

The children don't release him until Jen calls them in for a snack. "Well, you certainly made a big hit."

Damien shrugs. "You can thank my half-brothers for that."

Boy, when Damien turns off the stream of words, he shuts the faucet tight. "Were you out for a pleasure walk?"

"I wanted to get out of the house. I just heard that I got into Yale." Damien is looking out over the water. He's telling me something that matters to him, but he's not letting me close to him.

"Congratulations. But I don't think you can expect much sympathy for that." I reach out and touch his arm. He recoils.

"No, I guess not. Well, I have to get going."

He strides off down the beach, as if I'm contagious. I run up the steps and through the gate. Why did he have to come at all? He had no right in this world. I slam the gate, close the box, making it secure.

133

chapter 16

"Rachel, I want to talk to you." My father sits down in my desk chair, his arms crossed over his chest, his perpetually tolerant smile extended by lines of strain, like too many parentheses. He's come to tell me something unpleasant, to lecture me. I wonder if this is how he looks in his office, dealing with a recalcitrant student. Poor Dad. Unpleasantness isn't his thing. He belongs with obedient computers and smiling redheaded students.

"What are you doing to your mother? Do you know how upset you're making her?"

I look up from the bed and *War and Peace* to a Renoir print that's always hung on my wall—two girls sitting in a meadow. One dark-haired, one light. Julie and me. A soft world of lush lines and warm colors. Not like the lines of my mother's face—tight, thin, angry.

134

My mother has barely acknowledged my presence since I came home from Jen's this evening. At dinner, she spoke only to my father. I've found the secret of how to improve my parents' marriage. Just make my mother furious at me. I should send the tip to *Good Housekeeping.*

"I'm not doing anything to her."

"What's all this about spending the day at Mrs. Danby's when you're supposed to be finishing your applications?"

"I needed to get away."

"What you need to do is get those applications out. I don't understand you, Rachel. It's just a matter of putting some information on paper. Your mother even said you've done most of it already. Finishing up should be simple for you."

Simple for me? Simple for you. Things *are* simple for you, Dad. You have no problems with yourself. No part of you getting in your way, tripping you up, just plain sitting back and saying no. "I can't finish them."

"But why not? You should have no trouble with them. You're a bright girl."

My glance swings around on him, like a heavy crane. "Do you think I'm bright enough to get into Princeton or Harvard?"

"Of course. Didn't I tell you to apply to Yale?"

"But you know people at Yale. You're at Yale. How about those other schools? Would they accept me?"

"There's only one way to find that out, Rachel, and that's to apply."

That's not what I'm asking. I want to clamp his head

135

onto an optometrist's machine, enlarge his eyes until he sees only me. "But how do I compare with your students at Yale? Am I as smart as they are?"

"Well, don't forget that most of them are graduate students. They're a good deal older than you, so it's hard to compare. But I'm sure that when you're at their level, you'll do just as good work." Eyes shifting, voice smoothly reassuring.

Isn't that what parents always say? Wait, it'll be better later. I'm not asking for predictions of the future. I'm asking about me, now. "You mean I'm not one of your impressive types, like that new lady professor? My light isn't shining at seventeen?"

"Come on, Rachel, this has gone on long enough. The whole house is on edge. We've had enough of that."

That's what's getting to him. It's not what's going on with me. It's his own comfort that's being disturbed.

He gets up and pats my head. "Show me how fast you can get them done. You'll feel much better." He smiles. What relief. An onerous task over with. He's talked to me reasonably, and of course I will respond reasonably, like one of his students. Follow the law of supply and demand. He demands and I supply.

"Mom sent you, didn't she?"

"No, I came on my own, Rachel. I don't like to see your mother in this kind of state."

I pick up my book. It's not fair. He should have remained neutral. Well, I can withstand both of them.

The door has scarcely been closed a decent interval when my mother knocks. "Rachel, there's someone here to see you."

136

Someone? My girlfriends aren't "someone." Has Damien decided to try again? I open the door.

She steps into the room. "David is here."

David? I stare at her as though I can't make sense of her words. And I can't. David here? There's only the dark negative of his presence left, an empty, lonely spot.

However, it takes only an instant for the negative to be developed in full color, for me to feel my insides whizzing around like a Tilt-a-Whirl at full speed. My God, why did he have to come now? When my hair is as wild as Medusa's, and I'm wearing an old gray sweatshirt that's so voluminous it would take a boa constrictor to find a body under it.

"You have time to change if you want. He's with Daddy." So my mother's talking to me again. I guess the areas of our battle are neatly contained; school, yes; boyfriends, no. I can't chop up my feelings that way.

My mother leaves and I start pulling sweaters out of my drawer. The blue? The yellow? For some reason, I don't pick one of David's favorites. I go to the red turtleneck, already certified at Yale.

I brush my hair into a smooth, untroubled line. Two pimples sit like small volcanoes at my hairline, ready to erupt. I quickly loosen some hair and make a small dip over my forehead. Maybe that was the secret behind Veronica Lake's curtain of hair.

I brush on some rouge and paint my lips pink with Estée Lauder's Sunspiced Rose. How do I look? Mirror, mirror on the wall, do I look fairer than last fall? I don't know. It doesn't tell me. It's not the mirror that counts.

I take deep breaths as I go down the hall, smoothing

137

my insides, pulling in all the dangling wires. David doesn't touch me. He's removed from me, at a distance.

It takes exactly one look to erase that distance. Even in profile, David's dark beauty shoots right to my stomach. It's his eyes that do it. Last year Susan fell in love with a boy because of the way he crossed his legs. With me it's those dark, vivid brows, the long, curling lashes, like thick grasses along water; the black eyes, centers of gravity that pull everything into them. My composure doesn't even last me across the room.

"Hi, Rachel. How're you doing?" His voice is slow. He doesn't need to hurry. Everything comes to him.

"Fine." Just fine. Super. Why did you have to come back, just when I've gotten used to my diet? A dull, steady ache in my gut. Now you tempt me with sweets again. I walk over to the chair my father has just vacated, holding myself tight, straight, conscious of David's eyes on me.

"Well, it was nice seeing you again, David. Glad you're taking so well to Columbia." My father smiles his way out of the room. "Oh, Rachel, your mother and I have that cocktail party tonight at the Edmundsons, remember? Are you planning to go out?"

How do I know what I'm planning? I'm planning nothing. I'm planning everything.

"I was thinking Rachel and I might go to a movie, Mr. Gilbert."

"Fine with me."

Fine with him. Fine with David. How about me? My parents are probably delighted. They always approved of David. Polite, steady, going places. Sexy. No, that they

138

don't see. They probably think that I'll straighten out, now that David's back.

Are you back, David? Why are you here? What do you want? I only have to look at you sitting loose-limbed on the couch, smiling at me in that teasing, knowing way, to see what I want. I want to stay connected to your gaze, to feel special, chosen, at the center of everything.

But I can't show that. I have to be careful. I have to keep going, ignore the abyss of hurt, step over it. "What movie were you thinking of?"

"Oh, there're several goods one around. *Tootsie*, or *The Verdict*."

I nod, but I'm not ready to commit myself. I need some reference to all these months of waiting. I need something.

"So, you're liking Columbia?"

"So far. Everything but the food. I supplement my diet by going to parties. Even if I don't know anyone, I just sort of look at the ceiling and eat up the hors d'oeuvres. The fraternity parties are good for pretzels and chips and beer. Teas for visiting lecturers usually have good cakes. The cast party at the end of *Pirates* supplied a whole spread." David winks at me.

"Oh, are you singing in Gilbert and Sullivan again?" David, with his good tenor voice, gorgeous on stage. Always at the center of things.

"Yup, they let me in. I did Frederick."

The lead, of course. Surrounded by adoring maidens. "Do you ever do any work?"

David grins. "That, too. It keeps me busy most of the

time. The Applied Sciences school is tough, but so far I've done all right."

Our conversation is running along its old, usual lines. I ask, he answers. I demand, he supplies. There's usually little demand for my goods, except for a few polite inquiries.

"Good night." My parents pause in the doorway. "Don't stay out too late."

"Good to see you, David." My mother sends her smile only to him. She looks kind of refurbished, her light hair shining, her tall figure attractive in her old Persian lamb coat. So she wasn't planning to stick around to keep my nose to the grindstone. Maybe she's decided to let me slide to my destruction unhindered.

"Come over here," David says in his best gruff Humphrey Bogart voice, once my parents are out the door.

I sit stiffly on the edge of my chair. Why should I jump just because you call? Why should I come over? Other than the fact that that's exactly where I want to be.

I get up slowly. I'm going to be aloof as hell. I move languidly across the room, a sultry Lauren Bacall to his Bogart. Maybe I should tell him to whistle for me.

All he needs to do is reach out, and I'm over against him, feeling his hard arms across my back, looking into those bottomless black eyes. His face hovers over me, like his face one evening against a dark, velvety sky, his eyes and the night one.

"You look lovely, Rachel." He kisses me. I'm skinless, flooding into the air around me, dissolving. The familiar

140

firm lips, familiar musky smell and muscled body. Where I belong. I draw in lips, skin, scent. This is what's been missing. This was all that was wrong.

David lifts his head and grins at me. "We can continue after the main feature." He dips again and kisses my eyes, my nose, strokes my hair. Then he leans back. "We better go if we want to make *Tootsie*."

How can he be thinking of a movie? I don't move. I can't move. "I thought we hadn't decided."

"What would you like to see?" He pauses, willing to consider.

"David, you come in here like nothing's happened. Like you haven't been away for four months with no letters, no calls."

"Come on. We'll talk about it on the way." He stands up and extends his hand with a small grin.

I don't take it. I can't go to the movies like this, when nothing's been said. I can kiss him, but I can't go to the movies. It's crazy, but it's true.

"No, let's talk now. How can you just pop in after all this silence and expect me to act as if nothing's changed?"

David shrugs. "I just thought we were good enough friends to see each other once in a while."

"You mean you'll just drop in on me now and then, when you happen to be in the area and get the urge to see a hometown girl?"

"Now you sound like you did last summer, Rachel. I thought that after being apart, we wouldn't have to go through this every time. I explained that I don't want to be attached to anyone right now. I'm not ready for that."

141

"It wouldn't have hurt you to send me a note occasionally, or even call. That wouldn't bind you in undying fidelity."

David is standing still, no part of him extended toward me. "I felt it would be better to make a complete break. If I had written, you might have thought I didn't mean what I said."

"So what happened now? The New York girls aren't all you were expecting? You've been disappointed in love?" I hear the shrillness in my voice, but I can't stop.

David zips up his jacket. "Well, I guess this wasn't a good idea, Rachel. I'm sorry. I'd better be going."

I could still stop him. I could grab his arm and say that anything was better than his aching absence, that I would settle for whatever he was offering. But I don't. I sit there as he nods and turns away, as his green jacket disappears through the door, as his footsteps tap down the stairs. His car motor surges and then dies away into the lonely distance.

Everything is so still. The street. The house. It's like every particle of air is hanging separately. I run down the hall and curl up on my bed, hugging the pillow.

chapter 17

*I*t's Friday, December 31st. The last day of 1982. The end of the second year of Reagan's reign and the joys of supply-side economics. And the last possible day I can send out my applications.

My mother has not spoken to me for the past two days. She says nothing when I leave for Mrs. Danby's in the morning. She doesn't speak to me when I come home. She doesn't need to. The house speaks for her. Doors bang; pots clang; dishes rattle. Her footsteps are sharp, quick, angry.

I, on the other hand, move through this morning with deliberate slowness, choosing every activity carefully. To start with, I take a long hot shower, washing my hair. Susan is having some girls over tonight. Her boyfriend is out of town, and she doesn't want to be alone.

Who wants to be alone tonight? If I hadn't acted the way I did, I might have been with David on the eve of a new year. I twist my hair into my bath towel until my eyes tear, a counter to the pain inside.

I haven't heard from Damien either. Not that I should expect to. I've become an expert at shedding boyfriends.

In my bedroom, I lay out my clothes for tonight—a high-necked red blouse and beige pants. The garbage disposal shoots on in the kitchen, grinding loudly. It seems as though all the machines are going off at once—the disposal, dishwasher, coffee grinder. My mother is throwing all the switches, pulling all the plugs. But I ignore the house. I comb out my wet hair. Then I file my nails to pointed perfection and polish them a pinky brown. My surface will shine for the new year.

The sounds from the kitchen have ceased. Footsteps recede into the front of the house. I know what that means. My mother is indulging in her favorite escape. I can picture her lying there reading, but also listening, listening, trying to interpret the sounds from my room.

Well, I will give her no clues. I will be silent also. I prop myself up on my bed with my escape, *War and Peace*. Natasha at her first ball. The beginning of her romance with André . . .

I look at the clock. Noon. My stomach tells me that it's time to venture forth. I listen. All's quiet on the Gilbert front. Do I dare leave my bunker?

I walk quietly to the kitchen. Too late I hear the swift approach of steps. I duck my head into the pantry for

144

cover. My mother says nothing as she comes in. A cupboard near me opens and slams. I retrieve a can of tuna and turn toward the refrigerator. She has gotten there first. I stand behind her, dutifully waiting. Good little Rachel Gilbert, quietly standing in teacher's line.

My mother takes out a carton of milk and closes the door, turning away as though I'm not there. I reopen it and take out the mayonnaise. At the counter I mix my tuna and spread it on bread. My mother has taken her bowl of cereal to the kitchen table. I follow, sitting opposite.

She frowns into her bowl and eats with quick, sharp gestures. I take slow, deliberate bites, masticating thoroughly, as all the health books advise. I will stay my ground, show by neither glance nor twitch how the silence hurts, how effective this weapon is. I feel abandoned, orphaned. Is this the other side of all that love and preoccupation? Push it a little too far and it turns into enmity?

My mother gets up suddenly, bangs her bowl into the sink, and marches out of the room. The last twist of the knife. I am injured but alive. I take the remains of my sandwich into my room.

One o'clock. Only four hours to go. Four hours until five o'clock, the close of the post office, the close of all possibility. I want to stuff the remaining hours with activity, to leave no room for weakening.

I go over to my desk and dump the contents of a drawer on my rug. The end of the year is a time for sorting, disposing, paring down. That's what I seem to

145

be doing so efficiently, stripping myself of boyfriends, choice grades, choices. I might as well complete the process, rid myself of my whole past.

I sit down on the rug and start sorting. One small, stuffed bear David bought for me last spring at a fair. Out. An autograph book, filled with silly verses from childhood friends. Out. A diary from seventh grade charting my daily rises and falls in popularity, and my adoration of a slender, lean-faced boy with brains of mush. Out. A booklet of my first poems, all neatly typed and tied by my mother.

"Spring is near, spring is here, in its sensational career . . ." My period of throwing in big words without much regard to their relevance. "Through the vines in the twilight, nestled by the stream, cuddled under the moon's sweet gleam, with the sky as its shelter and the leaves for its bed, the little fawn was safe from its enemies' tread." I was big on animals and moonlight and trees. But I can't throw these out. They're part of me.

I go through other drawers, other writing. A mood piece written last year about a girl sitting outside her cabin at camp in the dark. "Nobody in the whole world knew she was out here. Not the other girls. Not the counselors. Not her parents, whom she used to feel would know everything important about her. An owl hooted, and it seemed to draw the ache out of her and spread it over the hills . . ." A humorous piece about a girl in a dilemma over buying a present for a mother who doesn't approve of Mother's Day yet still expects something, and ending up with a pair of underpants as the

146

most practical solution. They seem part of a distant past, when writing was more pleasurable, less complicated. When I could write at all.

I start to collect them, to place them neatly at the back of a drawer, all filed away. Completed. The complete works of Rachel Gilbert, ages seven to seventeen. My short, brilliant career.

The door to my room swings open. For a moment my mother sees me on the floor with papers around me, and her eyes fasten hopefully on my face.

"I'm straightening out my desk. It's a real mess."

Her face folds. *How sharper than a serpent's tooth . . .* "I see. Well, Rachel, you've done it. There's no way you can get anything mailed now. Whatever it is you've been trying to achieve besides ruining your life, I don't know, but you're certainly succeeding at that!" My mother slams the door shut behind her. The shelves along the wall vibrate, sending up puffs of white flakes, like snow signals.

The flurries subside. I subside, relax, let go. I'm a sentry relieved of her duty, a swimmer releasing her life preserver. I'm as still and calm as the gray sky outside my window.

The morning is washed clean, like the new year, rinsed of old patterns. I put on my robe and go out into the hall. My parents are still asleep. I start wandering through rooms. For the first time in weeks, I feel free to relax in them. I sink down into the soft cushions of the sofa.

A pale beam of sunlight falls on the green carpet, peaceful as a patch of sun on the forest floor. Specks of dust float idly in the light; I feel suspended along with them.

"You look very pleased with yourself." My mother sticks her head into the room, her face still creased with sleep, or with unforgiveness.

"Just feeling lazy."

"You mean you're not going over to your precious Mrs. Danby's today?" She turns and walks toward the kitchen.

After a few moments, I follow her. My mother is standing in front of the toaster oven, watching over a piece of toast. A sign that she's upset. Unlike most people, my mother can't eat when she's upset. She doesn't need fad diets to keep her thin, she has me.

I, however, am famished. Since I can see no indication of the presence of waffles, our usual holiday fare, I take down a box of Cheerios. "How was your party last night?"

"The usual New Year's Eve party. I could do without it." She does not turn around.

I take my bowl to the kitchen table and sit down. My mother butters her toast and stands at the counter, eating. She doesn't understand. There's no need for silence now. It's over. The whole thing was settled yesterday, at five o'clock. The battle's ended; it's the time for a rapprochement. But I can tell from her thin, unyielding back that she doesn't know this.

148

My father comes in wearing his old terry-cloth robe. "Happy New Year, everyone." He smiles hopefully.

"Happy New Year, Dad."

He sits down across from me. "Make any resolutions for the year?"

"She should resolve to find out just what she's going to do with herself next year." My mother's voice seems to be coming out of her sharp elbows, which jut toward us from the counter.

"She could wait until at least this afternoon to decide that." He reaches for the Raisin Bran.

"Well, if she's looking for an early morning activity, she could start by throwing out those applications that are littering her desk."

"What's the hurry? She might still use them." What's this? A last-minute gesture of paternal support? Or simply a refusal to accept defeat?

My mother whips around. "For what? There's nothing she can do with them now. She's made sure of that."

I feel like I've disappeared, been rendered invisible and voiceless by my rebellious act. And I suppose I'm not there for them anymore. Not the obedient, model daughter they thought they had. *I should be false persuaded I had daughters.*

I put my dish in the sink and walk out of the room. In the hallway, I pass Matisse's *Piano Lesson*. I pause. Why piano lesson? The picture is so still and silent there's no music in it at all. The boy looks lobotomized. Triangles of color jut into his face, partly obliterating it.

149

An intrusion of the gray and orange background into his head. A prisoner of the surrounding world. Something I understand, something I can write about. I go to my room for my notebook.

My mother comes down the hall, and stops, frowning. "What are you doing there?"

"Writing a paper."

"A paper about that picture? For what?"

"For English. Mrs. Baker asked me to do it."

"So now you decide to work, when it's too late." She walks past me, her arms held stiffly at her sides.

You have it backwards, Mother. It's because it's too late that I can work.

chapter 18

Mrs. Baker's arms sit on either side of my paper like two exclamation points. "So you think the *Piano Lesson* lacks music?" She gives me a pink-lipped smile.

All pinks and reds and whites. Hair gently curled around face, rouged cheeks, red silk blouse and white wool skirt. A regular Christmas package, one of Santa's helpers. Either she went to a super-deluxe spa over the vacation, or else her husband gave her an open-ended gift certificate to Elizabeth Arden.

Actually, I have another theory. I think I'm responsible. Standing up to me has done wonders for Mrs. Baker's self-image.

"Why do you say that?"

"Because everything's so still." I'll answer you, Mrs.

151

Baker. Why not? I've escaped you. You can't touch me with all the C's in China.

"And how does Matisse achieve this stillness?"

"With the large patches of color, all those straight lines, I guess."

"Yes, and how about some of the things you mention in your paper? The flatness, the balance, the way the mother in one corner is mirrored by the statue in the other. Don't those add to the stillness?"

"Sure." Agreeable Rachel. Amenable, amendable.

"Then tell me, don't you see the painting differently now that you've studied it? Isn't it richer for you?" She leans toward me, coming in for the kill, the telling twist of the lance.

I look at the gray, airy picture in my mother's art book, open on her desk. I look at Mrs. Baker's expectant face. "No. I saw all that before, just by looking at the picture. It makes me more conscious of what I'm seeing, that's all."

"All right, that's what I'm talking about." Mrs. Baker is nodding, full of enthusiasm. "Becoming more conscious of what you see in the painting, more conscious of what's going on in *Lear*. It makes us see things on many different levels. It adds depth. That's what's important."

No you don't, Mrs. Baker. You think you have me hanging there on the end of your lance, but you haven't pinned me yet. I'm faster than you think. "Everything that's important about the picture is right there on the surface."

Poor Mrs. Baker. I'm a stubborn case, I know. Deeply troubled, resists treatment. Why don't you place me in the incurable ward for those hopelessly out of touch with textual analysis?

Mrs. Baker sits back. I can tell by her steady gaze, her fingers tapping lightly on my book, she's not done yet. Raindrops falling on Matisse. She's regrouping, organizing another assault.

"All right, Rachel. What is it you see in the picture?"

"I see a boy who's imprisoned, by the piano, by the woman sitting behind him."

"That's not the way I see it. I see a very calm, peaceful picture."

"I think the calm is scary. All that order, and then the two triangles cutting into the boy's face. It's like he's no more than a piece of furniture, no more than the metronome on the piano."

"And I think the triangles link him to the scene in a pleasant way—they integrate him with the colors of the background."

Aha, she doesn't realize it, but she's played into my hands. I strike. "See, analyzing the picture just complicates things. It doesn't give any answers."

"I never said it did. It's a search for clues; you assemble them and draw your own conclusions. It's exciting, like detective work."

"I don't think it's exciting. It's dry, an exercise. It—" I look at the boy's lifeless face "—it lacks music."

That's it, Mrs. Baker. You used your best shot, and it missed me. Your ammunition is gone. Pull back your

153

hair, scrub your face, put on a sackcloth. You haven't converted me, after all.

But Mrs. Baker isn't slumped in defeat. She's smiling at me slightly. She actually looks like she's enjoying herself. "All right, Rachel, I can see I can't convince you. But as long as you're in my class, you'll do things my way. And my way is textual analysis."

I expect to feel the swell of anger, the hard edge of resistance. But I don't. It's a business deal. While you work for me, you accept my conditions. Either that, or you're out. It's a laying-your-cards-on-the-table statement of fact.

I nod and stand up. All right, Mrs. Baker. I can accept that. I don't have to like it and I don't have to pretend to agree with the method, but I'll sign to your terms. I'll do it because I'm a free agent. I can quit anytime I want. You see, I'm not afraid of the consequences.

Terry, just my luck, spots me coming out of the enemy camp. She squints. Does she sense conspiracy, collusion? "What were you doing in there?"

"Playing tiddlywinks." I start walking. Terry sticks by my elbow. She doesn't like missing the action.

"Did you do that paper?"

"Sure."

"Well, how'd it go? Did you stick it to her?"

"No. I agreed to do things her way." I turn, watching the effect of my words, Terry's rearing up. Eyes narrowed, head back, ready to strike.

"Afraid, huh? I should have known you'd cave in."

154

I stop. "Not afraid, Terry. I just thought it was fair."

"What does Mrs. Elitism know about fairness? She's really fair to Nina and Marjorie and to us."

"Well, I don't know. In some ways she's fair. She tries to be, anyway." Is this me talking? Speaking about my hated adversary, my wicked detractor? Something else occurs to me, which I couldn't bring myself to verbalize in a million years. She grades fairly. Your marks go up and down with the level of your performance.

"What'd she do, give you a love potion? There's only one person in that class she cares about, and that's Socrates."

"I don't know. I'm not so sure." She wouldn't have hauled me in, had that discussion with me, if she hadn't cared, right, Gilbert? That wasn't just for her own ego, that was for me too. "She just thinks what she's trying to teach us is important."

Terry's lips curl in a smirk, but she doesn't have a ready retort. Maybe she's considering this new language of mine. I don't wait to find out. "See you, Terry. There's something I forgot."

The kids for the next class are already coming in when I reach Mrs. Baker's room. "Could I talk to you for a minute, Mrs. Baker?"

She smiles at me with all the graciousness of her new look. "Well, the class is going to start in a minute, Rachel."

"That's all this will take. Remember those extra papers you said I could do? Well, I've decided not to do them."

155

Smile erased. Forehead creased. "I'm sorry you've decided that, Rachel. I think it was a perfectly fair offer."

"I don't mean it that way. I just mean that I don't want any special conditions. I'll take whatever grade I've earned."

She nods. "All right, Rachel, I accept that." She doesn't smile, but I can almost see the blood rushing around under her skin. I think I've given her a high to match any of Damien's.

As I leave the room, I take my emotional pulse. Where's the panic, the sense of doom? The shriveled, lost feeling? The scarlet C embroidered on my shirt?

What I feel instead is a swell of pride. I smile benevolently right and left. See me? I'm Rachel Gilbert. No special labels. No A-frame to hang my ego on. Just plain, unadorned. A person I might even get to like.

chapter 19

"What on earth was the point?" My mother draws her feet away from me on the couch.

"I had to tell her I wouldn't do them. I couldn't ask for special privileges." And I had to tell you. To make it complete, final, fini. So you'd have no more expectations.

My mother snorts. "You just had to ruin your record, is that it? To complete the damage."

"It was ruined already, Mom. I already got an F for a paper I didn't do."

My mother slams her book shut and swings her feet to the floor. "You're pretty proud of yourself, aren't you? Well, you won't feel so pleased with yourself next fall when all your friends are going off to college, and you're sitting home thinking about what you're missing."

"Maybe." That's a million years away. I just have to get through now. I stand up. "I'll have to see then."

"You'll have to start worrying about it a lot sooner, Miss. You'd better start figuring out what you're going to be doing." My mother stretches out again, as though the couch is now decontaminated.

I head for the door. "I need the car, Mom."

"Going to your precious day care? You'd better ask Mrs. Danby to put you on the payroll. If you think that your father and I are going to support you next year, you're dead wrong."

I run down the steps to the car. That's exactly where I was going. But suddenly I don't want to. I head the car up the hill. I'll go see Julie at the store. I'll see what it's like out in the real world.

At the jewelry counter opposite the front door of Hanover's, a saleslady with a puffy pink face stares blankly into space. Her scant hair hangs loosely down her back, like a teenager's, and she wears a tight black metallic sweater. I study her for signs of kinship. Can I read something about my future in her drooping face? I turn away.

Julie is in the infants' department, talking to two women. I walk slowly toward them. I'll wait until she's through.

"I'm just not sure how many of these infant suits we should take." The woman's brassy voice matches her large, busty figure.

"People say they're very useful," Julie says, almost shyly. "You could take some smalls and some mediums."

158

"That's not a bad idea." The woman turns to the other, younger one, and holds up a pink terry-cloth suit with a fat yellow duck appliquéd on the front. "Let's get this one, Letty."

Letty? I look more closely at the girl, with her back to me. Now I recognize the limp blond hair and thin shoulders.

"Okay." Letty shrugs. She sounds like it doesn't matter to her one way or another.

"Oh, hi, Rachel." Julie looks up and smiles. "I'll be through in a few minutes. Can you wait?"

"Sure. Hi, Letty." The girl has turned quickly toward me. She looks scared. She drops her gaze without answering and walks over to some baby blankets, fingering a blue-striped one.

I can't blame her for being uncomfortable. Two classmates are probably not what she bargained for in the infants' department. Maybe it makes her feel how far her life has swerved from the usual track.

I walk away. It's not my intention to spy. I should tell Letty we have something in common. We've both jumped the tracks, skidded off the line. Somehow, I don't think it would comfort her. And how much comfort can I find in her thin, defeated face?

I stop at a counter and pick up a soft blue and green plaid scarf. What am I thinking of? Purchasing a genuine wool scarf, when I'm about to become a pauper? I put it down. How does Letty do it? She gets pregnant, and her mother takes her shopping. I refuse to fill out a few applications, and my mother is ready to evict me.

159

"I just sold Letty's mother six stretch suits." Julie comes rushing up, putting on her coat. "Wouldn't you know they'd stick me in the infants' department? I have my dinner break now. Want to come?"

"You look terrific. Selling must agree with you." Suddenly I pick up the scarf and put it around Julie's neck. "Look, this is perfect with your coat."

Julie laughs and strokes the soft wool. I'm surprised she keeps it on. Clothes interest her only as a means of covering her body. "And how about this?" I grab a green beret and put it on her head at a rakish angle. "It picks up the green of your eyes."

Julie starts to take it off. "No, I don't need it. I have my old knit hat."

"But you do need it. It completes the picture. Take a look." I push her over to the mirror. I've found my calling. Rachel Gilbert, fashion coordinator. Rachel Gilbert, famous designer. No, no, not the right flair. Rochelle Jeelbear, with a French inflection.

Julie smiles slightly at herself in the mirror. The beret gives her round face a perky touch. With the fringe of blond hair and her delicate complexion, she looks like a lovely waif. "Well, maybe with the store's discount . . ."

"Go on. It looks great."

At the cash register, Julie takes the bag from the saleslady and walks briskly through the door. "You know, I was thinking that maybe I should buy some things for college next year, while I still have my discount."

160

"Good idea." My own animation is fizzling out. Is this how my mother promised I would feel next year? I don't look at Julie. She doesn't know about my applications.

"I might even see if I can extend the job past this month."

"But what about Mr. Phillips?"

"I could work for him during the week, and in the store on weekends. I haven't told you my best news. Mr. Phillips said that since I've been helping him so much with the book, he'd like to give me a percentage of the advance. He said it would be at least five hundred dollars."

"Is he going to make you co-author too?" Pretty soon the President himself is going to call up and offer Julie a loan. I feel as though she's slipping away from me, swimming farther and farther, toward the vanishing horizon.

"Let's go to Harry's. It's quick." Julie heads toward a small coffee shop. We sit in one of the four booths. A few people are at the counter—a heavy woman, a man with a visor pushed back on his head, and three elderly men.

Julie leans across the table and whispers. "Those three men come in every day at five and sit in the same seats and eat the same thing. I always hear the waitress ask if they want the usual."

I look at them. One is dressed in a suit and bow tie. Another, small and shrunken looking, chatters away while the other two eat. What's it like having your life so ordered that you don't have to make the smallest decision, not even which stool to occupy? "Maybe they have the secret of happiness."

"Three hundred and sixty-five meatloaves a year?"

"Maybe they don't have the secret for happiness."

Two girls come in, one tall and silky looking, the other chunky. They sit down in the back booth. "Isn't that Enid Burton, and Kate whatever-her-name-is?"

Julie nods. "I think Enid is at Miami this year."

"You should go talk to her."

"I don't want to bother her. Besides, Mrs. Daniels can tell me. She's visited the school."

"But this will be straight from the horse's mouth."

To my surprise, Julie gets up. "It'll probably turn out she's at the University of Arkansas."

I follow, feeling detached. A jellyfish, slowly undulating above the scene.

"Hi, Enid. I don't know if you remember me. I'm Julie Danby. I'm a year behind you at West Gate."

"Hi, Julie. What can I do for you?" Smooth. No comment on whether she remembers or not. Why should she remember? The lofty queen bee to the lowly worker. Actually, I'm impressed by Julie's directness in the face of those pretty, bland features, hair perfectly flipped back, ever so subtle blush-on and blue shadow.

"I was wondering how you're liking Miami? I applied there."

"Oh, it's great. Lots of fun."

"She particularly likes the social life." Kate smiles and winks. She has a wide, friendly face.

"What's to complain about?" Enid grins back. "Every-

162

thing's there, sororities, fraternities, billiards, bowl-ing—take your pick."

I have a sudden vision of crowds of new faces swarm-ing around, drowning out old connections, old hurts, making them not count.

"Oh, well, I was wondering about the work. Is it hard?"

"There's a lot of it, but it's a lot easier to do it under a palm tree in the sunshine than in gray old New York." Enid nods at Kate.

"How about the marine biology program? I've heard that's good."

"It's supposed to be. The Rosenstiel marine school has a separate campus, on Virginia Key. I think they even have research ships. But I haven't taken any biol-ogy. I'm in communications."

"The trouble is, you communicate too well. You should be in an all-girls' school. Then you wouldn't get so distracted," Kate comments.

"I don't want to lead the monastic life you do at Bar-nard."

"What's monastic? We can take courses at Columbia, and we have coed dorms."

"That's better than us. We have roommates, but they're all girls."

"Roommates? Are there suites?" Julie asks quickly.

"Nope. Not in the towers, where the freshman are. Two girls to a room."

"Are there any singles?"

"Only for upperclassmen, and that's by lottery. The

rest of us have lots of company—community bathrooms, one dining hall for both towers. You can't get lonely."

"Oh." Julie's face grows quiet, the way it usually does in company.

I glide down from my lofty height, filling in the silence. "What's Barnard like?" I turn to Kate.

"Well, it's a city school. It doesn't have palm trees and the ocean, but it has New York City and Columbia. I'm taking Oriental civilization and physics at Columbia next semester. That's a variety for you."

"Is your field physics?"

"I hope. It's tough. But the English department at Barnard is particularly good. Weren't you on the newspaper last year?"

I nod.

"They have a strong creative writing program. Lots of alumnae are published writers."

I'm no longer suspended, floating. I'm plunk down in the middle of my life. My stagnant, muddy life.

"Where are you planning on going next year, Rachel?" Kate smiles at me.

"Who knows?" I shrug. "Maybe China."

"What's this about China?" Julie asks as we return to our booth.

"Just wishful thinking," I say quickly.

Julie doesn't press. She's subdued during the meal. Sometimes she seems to be considering a spot way off in the distance. I don't mind. I don't feel so animated myself.

The night is solidly inked when we leave the restau-

164

rant. The street looks blotted out, its tinsel and neon candy canes darkened over the weekend. The dull beginning of a new year. Julie and I part at the door, and I cross the street to my car. A couple comes out of the hardware store and stops under the frosty lamplight. David, and Cindy Ferber, a girl from my class.

I stand motionless, looking across the car roof at them. She is talking animatedly, and he looks down at her with that amused half-smile of his. She is small, blond, bubbly. Not his old dark, serene type. I wish I could dislike her, but I can't. They worked in the store together last year, but she would never have gone out with him when he was my boyfriend. Now, obviously, he has explained how free he is, how unencumbered . . .

They start down the street. He puts his arm around her shoulders. I watch, until they are only dimly etched shadows. I jerk open the car door. Pain shoots through my hand as I jab my thumb into the handle. I slam the door, enclosing myself in the empty dark.

chapter 20

$\mathcal{K}$aren walked down the dark, still street. She pictured herself emerging from the cradling night into the bright lights and bright sounds of the party. It would be hard to cross over that line, but she would do it. She wasn't going to stay here in the dark."

I read over what I've written. I don't know why I've started writing again. I've done it without thinking, almost as a reflex. It doesn't seem to have anything to do with anything.

For the last few weeks, I've slipped through the days easily, not catching on their rough spots. I hear the kids talking about their plans for summer, their plans for next year, the senior prom, the end of school. None of it has to do with me. It doesn't seem like an ending to me. Endings mean beginnings.

166

Last year, I went to David's senior prom. What if Cindy takes him to ours? I see Cindy in the halls at school. She always gives me a cheerful, uncomplicated hello. But who's she kidding? There's nothing simple about our connection. She looks at me, wondering about my past with David, and I try to picture and not to picture their present. Has he gone back to school? It's the middle of January already. It seems funny for me not to know if he's in town. Like being left in the middle of a story.

Well, so what if she brings him to the prom? I won't be there. Who would I take? Damien? Damien would fit in about as well as E.T.

In school the next day, Damien actually condescends to walk down the hall next to me. Maybe he realizes I'm not going to attack him. I've accepted his distance. These days, I'm accepting almost everything.

"Still spending time at Mrs. Danby's seaside nursery?" He looks at me sideways, undecided whether to stick by me or skedaddle. At least he's not walking like a marine in review.

"Sure. Oh, and so are the swans. We seem to have become one of their regular stops."

"I hope not the only one. They're pretty big eaters. You really must like going there."

"I do. The kids are fun. And imaginative. You should see what they can do with a paper cup. Everything from using it as a telephone to eating it."

Damien laughs. A genuine laugh. It feels good. I

167

venture a personal query. "Have you adjusted to your future at Yale?"

"Yes, after a bout of self-pity. Actually, something you said helped."

"Something I said?"

"About making a life for myself at Yale. That I wouldn't have to feel like I was still stuck at home. And how about you? Where do you think you'll be?"

"Right here."

"Here? I thought you said you weren't going to Yale."

"I'm not going anywhere." I might as well make my situation public. It's no deep secret, is it? The truth is, Damien, that I'm the one who's stuck at home. To get away from it I tied myself to it. Ironic, no?

"What do you mean?"

"I didn't put in any applications. It's a little difficult to go somewhere when you haven't applied."

"But why not?"

"Because my mother wanted me to."

Damien gives a short laugh. He thinks this is a bit of Gilbert humor. He doesn't understand how unfunny it is. "What difference should that make? That's no reason not to go. You should be able to decide what you want."

Well, I've gotten what I wanted, Damien's attention. I've also gotten the irritating side effects. "What do you think I'm trying to do? Dance a jig?"

"I just think you're making a mistake."

"What's so terrible? Plenty of successful people never went to college." My skin feels tight, prickly. I didn't expect this straitlaced reaction from Damien.

168

"You're limiting yourself, that's all."

"Maybe I like being limited! Why are you suddenly so hot on formal education? I thought you despised it."

"Not colleges. That's different."

I don't wait to get a lecture on what I'll be missing. My mother can certainly handle that. I take off ahead of him through the sound barrier of the cafeteria, looking for a place to land where he can't follow.

"Is one of these for me?" I pull out an empty chair across from Julie.

"Sure. You seem in a hurry."

"Just escaping from Damien."

"I thought you had changed your mind about him."

"Well, he just changed it back for me. But what are you doing here? I thought you'd be helping Mrs. Daniels."

Julie looks down at her sandwich. "I haven't been there for a few days."

"No new projects for you?" My tuna sandwich oozes with sandwich spread. My mother started off the new year by declining to make my lunches. "How's it going at Hanover's? Did they agree to your staying on?"

"I don't know. I haven't asked."

"Doesn't the job end next week?"

"Yes. Guess who came in again yesterday?"

"Letty. That baby's going to be well supplied."

"I feel sorry for her. She seems so squelched. Her mother really bosses her."

"Maybe that's why she got pregnant, to escape from

her mother." Another avenue I might have taken. But then, there were no offers.

"Well, it doesn't seem to be working. It's just so sad. She's trapped."

I chew silently. There's another sad case across the table from you, I could add. A trapped, caged, limited friend. But I don't want to tell you. With Damien, the reaction was right there on the surface. With you it would sink like a rock, indigestible, undissolving.

"That's not something you have to worry about. What did Jen say about your book advance from Mr. Phillips?"

"She was happier about that than the money from Mrs. Daniels. That really gets to her. She considers it a handout." Julie's voice doesn't roller coaster. It just sort of grinds along the ground. I feel let down, flat. Something is missing. We are talking around each other, past each other. It's each other we're missing.

"I'm going to Julie's, Mom." I have perfected my technique. I drop my books on my desk, run into the bathroom, grab some pretzels from the kitchen, and dash out the door. I've gotten it down to three minutes. My mother doesn't even answer. I guess she doesn't care to comment on the further ruin of her daughter.

Jen greets me at the door. "I'm glad you came today, Rachel. Julie's home."

"She is? I thought she'd be at the store."

"She didn't go today. She's upstairs." Jen's round face looks drawn.

Julie unlocks her door. "Hi. Careful where you step."

170

Rows of starfish and shells and seaweed are stretched across the floor. There's about two inches of clear space to walk in. I tiptoe around the edges to the bed. "What's this? A seaweed rug?"

"Nope. I've decided to finally take charge of my overflowing collection and get it in hand. Look, the Danby collection." Julie holds up a stack of papers. The top one has sketches of all her starfish, from smallest to largest, five-armed perfection. She pats it. "My Echinodermata."

"How come you're not at the store today?"

Julie sits down on the floor among her possessions and starts to draw. Her skin looks flushed with the fresh air of the Sound. "I didn't tell you. I quit yesterday. It was too much, with Mr. Phillips."

"But I thought you wanted the extra money."

"Well, I may not need it now."

"Why not? Is Mr. Phillips handing over his entire advance?"

"No. It's just that I'm thinking of not going away to school." Julie looks up at me.

"I don't understand. Is Mrs. Daniels backing out?"

"No. But it was getting too complicated, taking money from here and there, and I would still have to take out a loan. I don't mind going to school around here."

"But everything was working out so well for you! Why would you give it up now? You can't do that!"

Julie smiles at my vehemence. "I can't go away, Rachel."

"Why not?"

She gets up and stares out the window. "I realized it when we were talking to Enid about Miami. How could I adjust to living with other people twenty-four hours a day? Everytime I think about it, I start to sweat. I couldn't stand not having my own room, a place to be by myself. That would be worse than what I have here."

"But maybe you could make some arrangement to live off campus or something. Don't give it all up just for that reason."

Julie shakes her head. "This is my place, right here. This room, this house, this water. I don't want to leave, Rachel."

"But you have to leave, don't you see? You have to be willing to try it!" Why do I feel so chilled? As though the air in the room has become thick and gray. Julie's words seem like echoes of other words. My mother's words.

"It's not so bad." Julie pokes me. "Don't look so forlorn. I'm not giving everything up. I'll be going to New Haven University."

"But I thought you wanted to go to a strong marine biology school. I thought that was the whole idea."

"Unfortunately, none of them are located in New Haven. Maybe I'll do well enough to transfer to Yale, or take courses there. And I'll be able to keep on helping Mr. Phillips with his book."

"You'll also be able to keep on entertaining three and four year olds in your house. Have you forgotten that?"

"But that's only nine to five, five days a week. I can work around that. I could still have my privacy."

I start to chew on my finger. "But what about Mrs.

Daniels? Have you told her? She's going to be pretty disappointed."

"I know. No, I haven't. That's the hard part . . ." Julie's voice fades away.

I look out the window. The Sound is gray and rippled, a constantly moving, changing picture. I remember winters when it has frozen clear out, a silenced slate of glass, the beach strewn with slabs of ice like glassy white whales.

"Well, in a way you're better off than I am. I don't seem to be going anywhere next year."

"What are you talking about?"

"I didn't apply to any schools."

"You're not serious! Come on, Rachel! You were applying to Princeton and Brown. That's where you wanted to go."

"Well, I didn't and I'm not."

"But why not? I don't understand."

You don't understand me. I don't understand you. I don't understand me. "That's where my mother wanted me to go. I don't know where I wanted."

"Oh, Rachel, what a waste! With your record, you could have gotten in anywhere. I thought that's what you were working for."

I look at Julie's dismayed face. It seems that she was counting on me for something also.

I turn back to the faceless Sound. As long as Julie was grabbing at life, it meant the possibility was there. It was like watching a boat's light bobbing in the night. But now there's nothing between me and the vast, unmarked water.

chapter 21

A stooped figure stands in the door of the classroom, talking to a larger figure. As I approach, the taller one breaks away. Julie hurries past me with a distressed look.

Mrs. Daniels turns slowly back to her room. Then she sees me and stops. "Rachel, come here a moment. I've never told you that I appreciate the job you did on the laetrile article. I thought it was well done." She sounds tired.

"Thanks, but Damien wrote it too."

"Well, the collaboration worked." She gives a weak smile. "Are you planning to do something with journalism next year?"

"I hadn't thought about it."

"No? Where are you applying?"

"I'm not."

The black eyebrows raise. "Then what are you planning to do?"

Too late now. "I have no plans."

"I see. Would you come into my room for a few minutes, Rachel? I have to sit down."

I don't want to follow her. I don't want to be that close to her, to sit alone with her. But I can't say no, not after her disappointment with Julie.

She sits down at a lab table, and I pull out a chair across from her. "So what's this about not applying to any schools, Rachel?"

"I'm just not sure what I'll be doing." I run my finger along the table's smooth edge. "I'm sorry about Julie, Mrs. Daniels. It was a surprise to me too."

"Ah." She closes her eyes. "It seems a shame, that's all, Rachel. She has such a natural interest in biology. It seems such a waste."

"But it's not all going to be lost. She's planning to study here."

"It's not the same. There are schools that are noted for marine biology. She should go to one of those. I've showed her some of the research that's being done. I gave her a book, *Lady With a Spear,* about a woman who's gone around the world as a deep-sea diver . . ." She lifts her hands. "Ah, well. Those are just the ramblings of an old lady."

"But she might still decide to do graduate work at one of those places. She still has time."

175

"I suppose." I know what she's thinking. That Julie may have time, but she doesn't.

"You still haven't told me why you haven't applied anywhere, Rachel."

What can I say? What I said to Damien, that it's because my mother wants me to? "It's just that it seemed—the only way out. What I was doing seemed to belong to everybody but me. I just wanted to find out what I wanted . . ." My voice fades uncertainly. I sound silly, like a petulant child.

Mrs. Daniels looks at me with her black appraising eyes. "It must be frightening, Rachel, to think you're going to do one thing, and then all of a sudden not do it."

I'm about to say no, that I'm all right, as I would say to any stranger. But the truth of her words hits me. All the scared feelings I've been trying to keep down spring into my throat. Yes, I want to cry, I am frightened. What's going to become of me? I've set myself outside the only future I can imagine. I'm left with no picture at all, only blanks. "It's just that I don't see any place for myself." My voice cracks on the words.

"Don't start thinking there aren't any alternatives. There's no one way to do things, Rachel. But reacting against something isn't enough. You have to take some sort of action. You know there are things you can do. Not all schools have an early deadline for applications. Or you could work for a semester, or even a year, as many students do, and maybe you'll feel readier to see what you want to do. Do you have any idea what that is?"

I stop. I've been asked all my life what I wanted to do, and I've never been sure how to answer. Do I know now, in this position, shaken loose from the web of my old expectations? Do I have the right to go find something just for myself?

"Well, I've always liked writing—creative writing, at least. And then lately I've been helping out Julie's aunt in her day-care center, and I've really been enjoying it. I don't mean that I want to be a nursery school teacher. I don't know what it means. Maybe something with child psychology, or children's development. And then there's math. It's always come easy, even though I'm not in love with it . . ."

Mrs. Daniels nods. "What it means is that you have to look around. Most of us don't automatically know what we want. We have to try things, take some chances, see how we respond. This is a time for you to search, Rachel. Don't be afraid to branch out and discover new things."

Her voice suddenly gets almost fierce. "But then when you find out, don't hold back. Go after what you want. There are no rewards in life for not trying. I should know."

I wonder what she is talking about, what it is she hasn't done. Is it what she hoped Julie would become? Is it that woman with a spear? I think of my mother.

"Well, I know you have things to do, Rachel. I can't keep you here all morning." She gets up from the table.

I stand up also. What she said scares me. She's not telling me what I should do. But she's saying that I can't

177

do nothing, either. She's sending me out to explore. Unlike my mother, she's giving me permission.

I go around the table and touch her arm. "Thank you, Mrs. Daniels." I realize suddenly what I've done, and I'm glad.

"To what do I owe the honor of having you in the house for more than five minutes?" My mother stands in my bedroom doorway. She looks brittle, almost frail.

"I have some things I want to do here, Mom."

"You mean you can stand being away from Mrs. Danby's for one day?"

"I want to look at some of these college catalogues and directories I got out of the library."

"This is a fine time to be looking at college catalogues!"

"It's not to apply. I want to see what programs and degrees there are. It might give me some ideas."

"Ideas aren't going to get you into school."

"No, but I need the ideas first, if I want to know what I'm going to do and where I'm going to go."

Suddenly my mother sits down on the bed and puts her hands to her face. "Oh, Rachel, what *are* you going to do? What's going to happen to you? I feel so bad for you."

I think of Mrs. Daniels and her crumpled expectations for Julie. I remember the energy she seemed to get from hoping things through her. For a moment, I get a sense of my mother's loss. I sit down by her and put my

178

hand on her back. "Don't feel that way, Mom. I'm going to be all right."

"How can you be all right? Where can you go?"

"Harvard and Princeton aren't the only schools in existence. I'm not exactly in exile or on the moon. There are plenty of good colleges that accept later applications. Or I can work for a while. I'm not going to mooch off you."

"That's not what I'm worried about, Rachel. I just said that because I was angry. What worries me is that you've lost all your good chances—"

"That's not so, Mom. I have the chance to look around and see what I, myself, really want to do. That's the important thing. You have to have faith in me."

My mother is looking at me with frightened eyes. It's a strange feeling, reassuring her. I feel a sudden sense of my own power. She wants to believe me. If I believe it myself, she will listen.

"I have to do it this way, Mom. I know it's right for me."

"I hope so." It's said in almost a whisper.

My mother gets up and walks slowly out of the room, leaving me alone with my choices. I pull over a college directory and open it.

chapter 22

"You may be interested to know that this is the last day we're discussing *Lear*." Cheers, claps. Mrs. Baker rests her small green-panted seat on the edge of the desk, smiling placidly.

"Today we're going to talk about the ending of the play."

"Then it should be a short class. It's simple. Everyone dies." Terry tilts back her baseball cap and grins.

"Not so fast, Terry. Back up a little. Since you're so eager to give an opinion, what's happening with Lear and Cordelia in the last act?" Mrs. Baker is becoming a regular student tamer.

"They waltz off to prison together."

"I'm talking about what's going on between them. Is Lear still unforgiving toward Cordelia? Rachel?"

Aha. I'm getting my one good solid notice per class. For which I perform dutifully. For some strange reason, curing my complex about Mrs. Baker has also cured my complex over Shakespeare. Like somebody who goes to a doctor for a cold and gets a headache cleared up in the bargain. Maybe, as Mrs. Baker so kindly pointed out, I just needed to pay more attention. Or maybe I'm just more relaxed, not so worried about what his words will bring me. Anyway, the awesome glow has dimmed. The words are spoken, flesh-and-blood words. Full of richness and beauty, but not holy vessels.

I flip through my pages, do my detective work, gather my evidence. Mrs. Baker, I know, will not accept unsubstantiated opinion. "Here, page one hundred twelve after Lear and Cordelia have been captured by Regan's and Goneril's forces, Lear says, *Come, let's away to prison./ We two alone will sing like birds i' the cage./ When thou dost ask me blessing, I'll kneel down/ And ask of thee forgiveness.* So he forgives her and wants her forgiveness."

"So Lear has learned humility. If you think of the play as the education of Lear, what else has he learned? Nina?"

My, my, coming to Nina early on, near the fresh opening of a class, not saving her for the stale end.

"Lear's learned to enjoy the simple pleasures. In the same stanza he says, *So we'll live,/ And pray, and sing, and tell old tales, and laugh/ At gilded butterflies.* He's content to stay with Cordelia in prison and talk and sing."

181

Mrs. Baker nods, smiles at her younger version. Nina's fawn face quivers with a smile. What a little encouragement will do. "That's right, Nina. And what else does this stanza tell us about Lear's evolution? Damien?"

Damien is practically stretched out flat in his chair. This is going to be a minimum-voltage, low-current job. "Lear says, *and we'll wear out,/ In a walled prison, packs and sects of great ones/ That ebb and flow by the moon.* He realizes that greatness and wealth are all transitory. The love and truth he and Cordelia have found are more important."

"And how about when Lear says, *And take upon's the mystery of things,/ As if we were God's spies.* What is he saying here?"

I see what he's saying. My hand shoots up, faster than a flying bullet, faster even than first-hand-up Cynthia. I'll take upon me the mystery, Mrs. Baker.

"Yes, Rachel?"

"It shows how much he feels outside of all the usual concerns of man. They'll try to understand the mystery of things, like God's spies. Spies are on the outside, watching, and God's spies are from another world. They're God's privileged, blessed with the sight and wisdom to understand the mystery of things."

Do I detect a slight glow emanating from the teacher? Could it be that I, too, have become a source of energy? Well, okay, Mrs. Baker, I'm willing to supply; I like to supply. As long as you and I know that, like Cordelia, I ask for nothing.

182